For more than forty years,
Yearling has been the leading name
in classic and award-winning literature
for young readers.

Yearling books feature children's
favorite authors and characters,
providing dynamic stories of adventure,
humor, history, mystery, and fantasy.

Trust Yearling paperbacks to entertain,
inspire, and promote the love of reading
in all children.

OTHER YEARLING BOOKS YOU WILL ENJOY

THE RISING STAR OF RUSTY NAIL, *Lesley M. M. Blume*

CORNELIA AND THE AUDACIOUS ESCAPADES
OF THE SOMERSET SISTERS
Lesley M. M. Blume

THE PENDERWICKS, *Jeanne Birdsall*

NORY RYAN'S SONG, *Patricia Reilly Giff*

HOW TÍA LOLA CAME TO ~~VISIT~~ STAY, *Julia Alvarez*

WHITTINGTON, *Alan Armstrong*

THE VARIOUS, *Steve Augarde*

PIECES OF GEORGIA, *Jen Bryant*

HARRIET THE SPY®, *Louise Fitzhugh*

VARJAK PAW, *SF Said*

TENNYSON

Lesley M. M. Blume

A YEARLING BOOK

Copyright © 2008 by Lesley M. M. Blume
All rights reserved. Published in the United States by Yearling, an imprint of Random House Children's Books, a division of Random House, Inc., New York. Originally published in hardcover in the United States by Alfred A. Knopf, an imprint of Random House Children's Books, in 2008.

Yearling and the jumping horse design are registered trademarks of Random House, Inc.

Visit us on the Web! www.randomhouse.com/kids
Educators and librarians, for a variety of teaching tools,
visit us at www.randomhouse.com/teachers

The Library of Congress has cataloged the hardcover edition of this work as follows:
Blume, Lesley M. M.   Tennyson / Lesley M. M. Blume.   p.   cm.
Summary: After their mother abandons them during the Great Depression, eleven-year-old Tennyson Fontaine and her little sister Hattie are sent to live with their eccentric Aunt Henrietta in a decaying plantation house outside of New Orleans.
ISBN: 978-0-375-84703-5 (trade) – ISBN: 978-0-375-94703-2 (lib. bdg.) –
ISBN: 978-0-375-84934-3 (e-book)
[1. Mothers and daughters–Fiction. 2. Dwellings–Fiction. 3. New Orleans (La.)–History–20th century–Fiction. 4. Depressions–1929–Fiction.] I. Title.
PZ7.B62567Te 2008   [Fic]–dc22   2007025983

ISBN: 978-0-440-24061-7 (pbk.)

Printed in the United States of America
10 9 8 7 6 5 4 3 2 1
First Yearling Edition

For Caitlin

CONTENTS

Part One

Chapter One

INNISFREE

Strange things had happened at Innisfree before. In fact, strange was usually normal at Innisfree. But what had happened the night before was a new sort of strange. A frightening, unsettling sort of strange, the sort of strange that nags at you when you try not to think about it and flickers behind your eyelids when you try to go to bed at night and won't let the sleep come.

Sadie hadn't come home.

The game of hide-and-seek had ended hours before, at dusk, as usual. At Innisfree, games of hide-and-seek took place in the tangled woods surrounding the shack on all sides, and they lasted all day. You could hide anywhere, practically. Up in a tree; behind a thorny bush; in a hollowed, burnt-out stump. You could even bury yourself in the dirt and leaves and wait there for hours, breathing in the musty smell.

But there were rules too. Rule number one: you couldn't hide in the river. The river might look cool and inviting, but it was filled with tricks and temptations and secret dark swirls that would grab a little girl around her ankles and pull her down to the bottom.

"Look down, but don't lean over too far," Emery had warned his girls one day as he paddled them along the river currents in the rowboat. "Just far enough to catch a glimpse."

A glimpse of what, Tennyson and Hattie had asked their father.

"The little girls at the bottom of the river," he answered. "That's what the Mississippi does. It tempts you in, and then it catches you. It loves you and doesn't want to let you go. So it pulls you down to the bottom and keeps you there. If you look down, you'll see the faces of the little girls who didn't listen."

"I see one," cried Hattie, who was only five at the time, pointing down at the water. "She's staring up at me! Oh, can't we reach in and save her?"

Emery laughed. "That's just your reflection," he told her.

And how was Hattie to know? There were no mirrors at Innisfree. No pictures, no paintings, no way to see what you looked like, except when others described you back to yourself. The only reflections at Innisfree were words.

So, that was one of the rules. That the Mississippi was

hungry, and would resort to all sorts of intrigues to trap you in the dark, silty stillness at the bottom for eternity. That's why no one was allowed to hide in the river.

Another rule: the game was over at dusk. Always. Because you never know what could happen to you in the woods after dark. So when the sun began to sink down low over the river and the air around you started to turn purple-gray and the lightning bugs hung like fairy lights in the haze, it was time to go home. You would come out of hiding. You would pad barefoot through the trees, slapping mosquitoes away from your ankles, until you saw the damp yellow light of the oil lamp on the porch of Innisfree.

Everyone knew these rules. Which is why Tennyson and Hattie grew worried when their mother, Sadie, hadn't come home at sunset.

"What if the river caught her," Hattie whimpered. "What if she's stuck down there at the bottom, with all of the little girls who didn't listen?"

Emery sat on the stairs of the front porch and stared out into the black woods. The right side of his sweaty face glistened in the light of the lamp. He didn't say anything.

"How will we get her out of the river?" pressed Hattie, who was eight years old now.

"I don't know, baby," Emery said.

Tennyson, who was eleven, sat cross-legged on the far end of the porch, just outside the ring of yellow light, in the sticky black shadows. She watched her father, who was rocking ever so slightly, as though lulling an invisible baby to sleep. His lips moved and he was saying soundless words. But he wasn't talking to Hattie. And he wasn't talking to Tennyson. He was having a conversation with someone who wasn't there.

"She's not in the river," Tennyson said. "And this isn't a game. She's gone away, hasn't she."

Emery stood up and brought the girls inside. "Go to sleep," he told them, and turned off the oil lamp. "I'll be back in the morning."

Moths danced on the screen of the girls' bedroom window. It was too hot for sheets. It was too hot for nightgowns even. It was so quiet that Tennyson could hear her own heart pounding.

"Tennyson," whispered Hattie, even though there was no one there to scold her for being awake so late at night. "Tennyson."

"What is it?"

"I can't sleep. Let's go on the swing. Papa'll never know. He won't be back till the morning. He said so."

"All right."

They turned the key in the oil lamp in the main room, and warm, reassuring light washed over them. This reminded Tennyson of wetting the bed, when you would wake up to a feeling of odd warm comfort and terrified guilt at the same time.

A thick rope, knotted at the bottom, dangled from a rafter above. A different family would have had a dining room table in the middle of that room. But the Fontaine family had a rope swing instead. Tennyson let Hattie take the first turn. Her little sister's body looked like a fine white fish, clinging to the rope and sailing through the air.

"Push me!" shouted Hattie. Tennyson gave her an extra-hard shove and cringed as her sister hit the far wall with a thud. Several sheets of paper that had been tacked to the wall fluttered to the ground.

"Sorry," said Tennyson.

"It doesn't matter," said Hattie from the air. "One more bruise won't make a difference." She was right. Blue-purple bruises and scratches covered her legs and Tennyson's too. The bottoms of their feet were as thick as hides from running barefoot in the woods all the time.

Tennyson tacked the yellowing papers back up onto the wall. Poems and stories had been written on these papers. Sadie, their mother, was a poet and a story writer, and she had written them. Usually the room felt noisy with all of these words shouting from the papers on the walls. But tonight a tomblike quietness filled the room and throbbed in the corners. Tennyson looked at the poems and stories and missed her mother. But she knew that Emery missed Sadie even more. Her father was a strong man. Sometimes it seemed to his daughters that he didn't need food or even water, but he needed Sadie. Even Tennyson knew that, and she felt terrible for him.

The girls took turns on the swing until Tennyson's head began to swim with tiredness. They had used up almost all of the oil in the lamp, and the room was hot, like somebody's breath.

The black began to drain from the sky in the east, and still Emery didn't come home.

Tennyson and Hattie curled up around each other like foxes on their bed and fell asleep. Then the faded calico curtain in the door moved and Emery was in their room. Sunbeams danced around his head, with its damp short curls, and he sat on the edge of their bed.

"Your mother's gone," he said.

"Where?" asked Hattie.

"I don't know," he said, his head in his hands. "I looked for her all night. I need to find her. And you can't stay here alone while I'm gone looking. Pack up some of your clothes."

Tennyson sat up in alarm. "But where are we going?"

Her father looked at her blearily. "To Aigredoux," he said.

And he walked out of the room.

✦✦✦

Aigredoux.

It sounded like a kind of candy. Something that would come in a cardboard box with bright colors on it, maybe a rainbow. Something that would melt on your tongue and stain it bright pink.

But Aigredoux wasn't a candy. It was a house. And its name told you all you needed to know. Emery said that Aigredoux meant "bittersweet." He should know; he had grown up there. Along with his sister and his brother, the one who died in the big war. All of the Fontaines had grown up there for generations.

Except for Tennyson and Hattie. They had never been to

Aigredoux. They had grown up in their shabby little house on stilts in the woods. In Innisfree, far away from Aigredoux, with only Sadie and Emery and the trees and the river around them and no one else. There was their dog, Jos, too. But Jos almost didn't count because he didn't really belong to them. He was wild. Sometimes Jos didn't visit Innisfree for days, and then he would casually show up for breakfast. Or dinner. He was wild, but he would always lick his paws before coming into the house, because he was a gentleman. And then, when he was done and settled in, Emery would ask him:

"So, Jos, where've you been?"

And Tennyson and Hattie would take turns making up stories about the latest expedition of Jos in the woods. Tennyson was especially good at making up stories, and not just about Jos either. She just understood people and how things worked and it showed in her stories.

In fact, this made Sadie jealous sometimes, the fact that Tennyson was so good at stories. The characters in Sadie's stories never seemed to behave themselves. There was that time when Sadie wrote the story about a French family during the big war in Europe, for example. She worked on it for many days and many nights in the room with the rope hanging from the rafter, spreading the pages across the floor and getting mad when her characters misbehaved.

One afternoon, she surrendered and took a nap in her bedroom, her ink-stained hands pressed together and tucked under her face while she slept. Tennyson tiptoed into the main room and read the words on the strewn pages on the floor, but what her mother had written didn't make any sense to her. People didn't really behave that way, the way that Sadie had written.

An hour later, Sadie woke up, the late-afternoon sun stinging her eyes. She padded back into the main room and found Tennyson calmly writing on the strewn pages.

"I think I fixed your story," Tennyson said.

Sadie stared at her daughter and a second later, she was on her knees, snatching up all of the pages, clutching them into wads, like big shredded camellias. She held them to her stomach and bawled until Emery came in and held her and made Tennyson go outside.

After that, Tennyson only wrote and told stories about little girl things, like Jos. Writing about big things was Sadie's dream, and she had put a barbed fence up around it. So Tennyson stayed away.

***

Emery said that Jos couldn't come along to Aigredoux. The girls didn't even get to say goodbye, because Jos was off having another adventure and he didn't know yet that Sadie hadn't come home.

Hattie cried as she lugged her bag into the front seat of the truck. "But what will happen to him?"

"Jos can take care of himself," said Emery. "There are lots of birds and squirrels for him to eat up, and he can sleep under the porch when he feels like it. He'll be fine."

He locked the front door. Tennyson wondered why he bothered, since there was no glass in the windows of Innisfree. Only screens, some with holes the size of apples. Anyone who wanted to get into Innisfree could just go right in. But Emery locked the door anyway.

The road along the river was bumpy and Tennyson and Hattie pressed their feet against the dashboard to brace themselves. Gradually the woods thinned out and then the hot sun beat down on the roof of the truck. Dust swirled in through the open windows. Hattie, who sat in the middle, rubbed her tongue with the hem of her dress.

"The dirt keeps getting in my mouth," she complained. Hattie never breathed through her nose. Her lips were always cracked from breathing through her mouth.

The truck rolled out of Mississippi and into Louisiana, and as far as Tennyson could tell, there was no difference. She looked at the people they passed on the side of the road. They were poor people. Emery said that everybody in America was poor these days. It was 1932, during the Depression. Fresh eggs were a luxury. Diamonds were a dream from another world. No one had any money. Things were evening out among people everywhere.

But these people on the river road in this part of Louisiana had to be very poor. A woman washed her baby in a muddy puddle. A swarm of children tore at a chicken carcass, even eating the bones.

"Papa, are we poor?" Hattie asked.

"Yes, baby, we're poor," Emery answered.

"Are we as poor as these people?"

"Almost."

"But I thought that Mama said our family used to be rich," Hattie said.

"They were rich," said Emery, staring vacantly through the windshield. "But it was blood money. I'd rather be poor. And it's all gone now anyway."

"What's blood money?"

"Let Papa concentrate on his driving," he told her.

Tennyson was quiet. She let Hattie ask all of the questions, as usual. Sadie used to say that Tennyson doled herself out in teaspoons while Hattie heaped herself on like a pile of sugar.

"You're my watchful, wise owl," Sadie would tell her. "With an old soul. But your sister is my heartbreak. There're no walls around Hattie to protect her. So it's up to you to take care of her."

So Tennyson let Hattie ask the questions, and instead of asking questions herself, she listened to the answers from behind her own wall and silently looked after her sister.

Tennyson watched the poor people by the side of the road, but she saw right through them. They were like ghosts to her. She could look through them and see trees and grass and shacks on the other side. All she could think about was the fact that her mother was gone and soon Emery would be gone too and that she and Hattie were going to Aigredoux. The house that was like bitter candy, a strange poison-like candy that stayed in your blood once you ate it.

"How long will you be gone?" Hattie asked Emery.

"I don't know."

"Where did Mama go?"

"I don't know."

"Why did she leave?"

"I don't know," said Emery.

They were all quiet again, until Tennyson said:

"I know why she left."

Emery looked at her. "Why?"

"Because she's like Jos," answered Tennyson. "She's wild and she doesn't really belong to us."

That was the first time the girls ever saw their father cry.

Chapter Two
THE COLORLESS TEMPLE

One time a visitor had come to Innisfree. Sadie and Emery were poor but they were Southerners, which meant that they always made room for one more in the house.

This visitor was a man named Christian, an old friend of Sadie's from New Orleans. Tennyson had been six at the time, and Hattie was three. The night Christian arrived, they all ate dinner on the porch in the yellow light of the lantern and watched the fireflies glimmer in the black air.

After dinner, Christian smoked a cigarette and leaned back against the house. He looked at Sadie.

"You should be famous," he told her.

"You're just saying that," Sadie said modestly, but she

blushed with pride. Tennyson saw the girlish blush and felt a swell of embarrassment for her mother.

"No, I'm not," said Christian. "I swear. Someday you're going to be famous as Emily Dickinson or Virginia Woolf. We'll see your poems and stories splashed across the pages of the *Sophisticate* in no time."

The *Sophisticate* was an important magazine that published the best writers in the country. Sadie read all sorts of things like that. Somehow a dozen magazines managed to find their way to Innisfree every month. But the *Sophisticate* was her favorite, and it made Sadie happy that Christian thought her stories should get published there. Because if one of her stories got picked, that would mean that Sadie was officially a great writer.

But what Sadie didn't tell Christian was that she mailed stories to the *Sophisticate* all the time. Every few weeks she would send off a story and pray, but she never did get picked. This was very hard on Sadie, and that's why she hid this shame from the visitor who told her that she deserved to be famous. Instead, Sadie just drank up his praise like sugar water.

"Yes, ma'am," said Christian, lazily blowing smoke into the air. "You'll be one of the greats. As long as you can find time to write . . ." His voice trailed off and both he and Sadie looked at the girls.

Emery snatched up the dinner plates.

"Come on, girls," he said. "Let's clean up and play on the swing."

Tennyson and Hattie followed him inside. But Christian

and Sadie stayed on the porch for a long time, smoking and watching Sadie's dream shimmer and billow in the nighttime haze.

✦✦✦

Christian had been fascinated by Tennyson.

"How old are you?" he asked her one morning.

"Six."

He stared at her. "I've never seen anything like your eyes," he said. "They change all the time. One moment they're blue and then they're green. It's like they don't want me to know what color they are."

"Maybe they don't," said Tennyson.

"You're the oldest six-year-old I've ever seen," he said, almost warily. "So serious."

That was true enough. Tennyson had always been serious, probably because she'd always had serious work to do. Sadie and Emery had been very young when Tennyson was born and they didn't know how to be parents when she came. They had only been playing house when they discovered that she was coming. Innisfree had been like a tree house or a backyard tent—a place of make-believe. Although instead of playing games they had been playing at being grown-ups. Even when Sadie's belly grew as big and round as the moon with Tennyson inside, they still just went on playing house.

So when Tennyson finally came, it was her job to teach them how to be a mother and a father.

Emery and Sadie didn't always get things right. When baby Tennyson was hungry, she would have to cry to get their attention and tell them so. Often when Tennyson cried, Sadie cried too. And then one day, Emery came into the house and Tennyson was crying on her blanket and Sadie was just sitting there in a corner, staring into space.

"Didn't you hear the baby?" Emery asked. He looked more closely at his wife. "What's the matter with you?"

Sadie went on staring at sunbeams.

"I'm nothing," she said. "I don't matter anymore."

"What are you talking about?"

Sadie still wouldn't look at him. "It's over."

"What's over?" asked Emery.

"There's only the crying, all the time, nothing else. I'm never going to write again. I'm nothing. I might as well not exist."

Emery picked baby Tennyson up and hugged her protectively to his chest. From then on, he took care of Tennyson, and when Hattie came along three years later, he took care of her too.

So Sadie got to go back to being a poet and a writer and then she stopped staring at nothing and saying things like "It's over." And then, when Tennyson and Hattie stopped being babies and started growing up, Sadie even almost seemed happy again, because once in a while she could see the poetry in raising untamed little girls in a shabby house on stilts in the woods, with poems and stories tacked to the walls and a rope swing in the main room and a wild dog named Jos with good manners.

Of course, she never *wrote* about Innisfree. She only wrote about big things that she knew nothing about, big things happening to strangers. The small, petty poetry of her family was like a fence to be peered over. It was a dishpan of dirty water and she wanted the ocean.

But in any case, Tennyson worked very hard to make sure that Sadie continued to see the poetry in life at Innisfree. That was another one of her jobs that she took very seriously.

Because she knew, even as a little girl, that the minute her mother didn't see the poetry in her family anymore, Sadie would be gone.

❖❖❖

The air changed as the truck rolled closer to Aigredoux.

Tennyson pinched her nose shut with her fingers and blew, hoping that her ears would pop. They didn't. The pressure just kept building up. A storm was on its way across the river. They were in sugarcane country now. Innisfree was in cotton country. It was on higher ground, on the bluffs far above the Mississippi. But down here, on the Louisiana river road, the soil was too damp to grow cotton. Sugarcane was king. White gold, they'd called it in the old days.

It was the end of the summer and the cane had grown tall. Earlier that afternoon, dust had swirled around the roots of the cane, but now there was no wind and the dust stayed on the ground. Thousands of lines of emerald green cane stretched to the horizon on the left of the truck. To the right of the truck ran an endless levee, a tall man-made ridge of grass-covered land. The levee was supposed to keep the Mississippi at bay, to keep it from surging out of the riverbed and savaging the sugarcane and the houses in the middle of those emerald-colored fields.

But everyone knew that the Mississippi did as it pleased. If it felt like pushing the levee right out of the way, it did. Sometimes it swept away a whole field of cane. If it was particularly hungry, it might swallow up a whole house. This didn't happen very often. Most of the time the river was lazy about the levee. But once in a while it would surge up just to remind everyone who was boss. Sugarcane was only king when the Mississippi allowed it to reign.

"We're almost there," Emery said.

Tennyson looked at her father. She thought that he was beautiful. There was something about him that always made people act respectful. Even when his neck was sweaty and his face was dirty and he had two wild little girls with hide-thick feet sitting next to him in a rattling old truck.

"I want to talk to you about Aigredoux," he said.

"Okay," said the girls.

"Your aunt Henrietta lives there," he said. "She's my sister, and she'll take care of you while I'm gone. I want you to mind her. Even if she's not like me or your mother."

"What do you mean?" asked Hattie.

"Your aunt lives very differently than we do at Innisfree," said Emery. "And she sees life very differently too. While you're at Aigredoux, I want you to pretend that you're in a play. If Aunt Henrietta asks you to behave a certain way, pretend that you're actresses and that you're being given a part."

"How will she want us to behave?" Hattie asked.

"Like ladies," Emery said flatly.

"How does a lady behave?"

"Like Aunt Henrietta," said Emery. "I want you to be brave. I'll come back as soon as I can and we can go back to Innisfree."

Tennyson pondered the riddle of acting like Aunt Henrietta when Aunt Henrietta was as much of a mystery to her as God. She wondered what Jos was doing at that moment. Or Sadie. Or the little girls at the bottom of the Mississippi. She caught herself wishing that she was one of them, dwelling down there in the warm, silty dead familiarity, in a place where no one could leave the others.

❖❖❖

The sky over the river was bruise-colored, but over the cane fields the sun still shone down through the clouds in piercing gold shafts. Thunder rumbled in the distance, a listless, grudging sort of rumble that soothed and threatened at the same time. No one was in the fields and no cars drove along the river road. At that moment it seemed to Tennyson that she and Emery and Hattie were the only people alive in this strange hot world of ripe cane and purple river and listless thunder.

"I want to get out," Hattie whined. "I'm tired of being in this hot truck."

She stuck her feet on the windshield. When she moved them again, a steamy white outline of them stayed on the glass. Ten little steam circles where ten dirty little toes had been.

Emery steered the truck off the road onto the grass.

"Look over there," he said. He pointed to a dense grove of tall, thick, ancient-looking trees in the middle of the cane field. "Do you see what's in the middle of those trees?"

Tennyson squinted. "A huge house," she said.

"Does anyone live there?" asked Hattie. "It looks kind of broken down."

"That's Aigredoux," said Emery. "That's ours."

"Is all of this ours?" exclaimed Hattie. "All of these fields and everything?"

"Not anymore," said Emery. "Aigredoux used to be a huge plantation and all of these cane fields belonged to it. But the fields were sold off to a big company a long time ago. Now Aigredoux is just the house and the front and back yards." He turned the key in the ignition and the truck shuddered and died.

"We're walking there?" Hattie asked. "Why can't we just drive?"

"You'll see why in a minute."

Tennyson got out. Her legs ached and her spine throbbed from being jostled around in the truck for hours. The sharp edges of the grass sliced at her ankles and legs, like paper cuts.

Emery pulled the girls' tattered duffel bag out of the back of the truck.

"Follow me," he said.

Soon they stood in front of a thicket of vines.

"Look at this," Emery told them, nudging aside one of the vines with his foot. Underneath lay a carpet of pale smashed shells. "This used to be the driveway to the house," he said. "Watch out for snakes."

Hattie began to cry. Hot tears cleared pink trails down her dirty cheeks.

"I want to go home," she said.

Emery swung her onto his shoulders and forged the way up what had once been the bright, smashed-shell driveway.

Tennyson's heart pounded as she followed him. She said the name of the house over and over to herself. *Aigredoux, Aigredoux.* She drew out each syllable until it sounded like a children's song, something less scary. *Aaaag-rehhh-do.*

Trees grew on either side of the driveway and they reached across and intertwined branches to make a long, dark tunnel. These trees were as lazy and heavy as the air. Instead of reaching up toward the sky, the bottom branches of Aigredoux's trees lay across the ground. Tennyson almost expected them to yawn and wake up and stretch their branches toward the sky where they belonged. But they didn't wake up; they just kept sleeping their drugged slumber. Thick gray Spanish moss hung from every branch, sullenly drinking up the light and looking like ghost clothes that had been flung up there to dry.

Aigredoux, Aigredoux.

As they walked through the tree tunnel, the house at the end rose up out of the ground and the trees seemed to part. And suddenly there they were, the three of them, standing in the shadow of Aigredoux.

"It has no color," said Tennyson.

"What?" said Emery distractedly.

"The house," said Tennyson. "It has no color. Like a mirror or a lake on a cloudy day." She had never seen a colorless house before. Even their dirty little house on stilts at Innisfree had a color. It was brown, like sticks, like kindling being put into a fire.

But Aigredoux towered over them like a huge, colorless temple, as though history had drunk up all of its color and left it an empty glass. It might have been made of ice. The dark windows stared down at them like dead eyes. Thick vines grew in a tangled web up the plastered walls.

The front door of the house opened and a woman came out. She didn't see Emery and Hattie and Tennyson standing there. They watched as she reached out and seized a vine that snaked up along the doorframe, gripping the wall with its vicious roots. The woman tugged, but the roots appeared to be winning. But then came a ripping noise and the vine released its grip and fell to the porch like a heavy rope. The woman had won, but the vine had the last laugh. As it came off the wall, it tore out chunks of colorless plaster, which fell like an avalanche of snow onto the woman.

Hattie laughed and the woman on the porch spun around.

The look on her face would have stopped a bullet. Hattie's laugh froze in midair. It fell to the ground and shattered like an icicle.

"Henrietta," called out Emery.

The woman drew in her breath and straightened up. She towered, like the columns on the temple where she lived.

"Wait here," said Emery, placing Hattie on the ground. He dropped the duffel bag too. The girls sat on it as Emery marched across the lawn toward the towering woman. When he reached the house, he had to walk up a wooden plank that had been placed over the broken front stairs. Then he was standing in front of his sister.

"I wish we could hear what they were saying," said Hattie, her cheeks still striped from her tears. She looked like a little pink and brown tabby cat.

Emery gestured to the girls to come up onto the porch. The woman stared down at them.

"I have never seen filthier children in my life," she said.

Tennyson went numb. Hattie sank into her side and her sticky little hand clutched Tennyson's.

"They're just little girls," Emery said. "Don't make this even harder for them." He came down the plank and knelt in front of them.

"This is your aunt Henrietta," he told them, as if they didn't know. "Remember what I told you about this being a play. Aigredoux is your stage. I'll be back soon. With your mother."

"What kind of a mother leaves her husband and her

children?" spat Aunt Henrietta. "Just let her go, Emery. I told you that you never should have married that woman. And you did and now here you are, on your knees. Right where I told you you'd be."

If Emery was listening to her, he didn't show it. He kissed Hattie on her damp tabby-cat cheek and Tennyson on her forehead, and then he left.

Aunt Henrietta watched him go, her lips moving silently. The way she did this reminded Tennyson of Emery's talk with himself the night before, on their rickety porch at Innisfree. When Emery's truck had gone, back up the river road, swallowed by the fields of emerald green cane, she looked down at Hattie and Tennyson.

"There's no escaping facts," she said after a minute. "Your father should have known better when he left. Aigredoux *always* calls the Fontaines back. Follow me."

And she disappeared into the dark front hallway of the colorless temple that was now their home.

Chapter Three

ZULMA

The main hall inside was very dark and their eyes had to adjust. Slatted shutters covered the windows, casting slashes of brackish sunlight on the floor. Rows of paintings hung on the walls and the faces in those paintings stared down at Tennyson and Hattie.

"Who are they?" Hattie asked, pointing.

"A lady *never* points," snapped Aunt Henrietta. "This hallway is known as the Hall of Ancestors. The people in these paintings are Fontaines, going back five generations. And they would all be as appalled by your appearance as I am. You look like paupers in those rags and with those dirty little paws."

"Papa says that everyone is poor these days," said Hattie.

"You are not *every*one," Aunt Henrietta told her. "And from now on, you may only speak when I require an answer. Stand up straight and tell me your names."

"I'm Hattie," said Hattie.

Aunt Henrietta nodded with approval. "That was your great-great-grandmother's name," she said. "And you?"

"Tennyson," said Tennyson.

"Oh, *please,*" said Aunt Henrietta. "How typically bohemian of your mother to name her daughter after a poet. Follow me upstairs. I'm putting you in Louvenia's room."

"Who's Louv–" Hattie began, but Aunt Henrietta's sharp look froze Hattie's voice.

A grand staircase swirled up from the Hall of Ancestors to the second floor.

"Walk only on the left side," Aunt Henrietta told them. "The staircase is under construction."

She started up the stairs, her back as straight as a cadet's. A plank covered one end of the third stair and the girls stepped over it.

"Zulma fell through in that spot yesterday," Aunt Henrietta said.

"Who's Zulma?" asked Hattie, but of course she did not get an answer. Halfway up the grand staircase, the stairs stopped being made of rotten wood and started being made of cool pale marble.

"Don't go in that room," said Aunt Henrietta, waving her hand in the direction of a closed door at the top of the stairs.

"It's under construction. That one is under construction as well," she added, pointing to another door.

Hattie tugged on Tennyson's dress. "Why are all the door locks upside down?"

"I don't know," Tennyson whispered back.

At the end of the upstairs hallway stood a tall window leading onto a porch. If you stood on this porch, you could look out over the tops of the gnarled trees on the front lawn of Aigredoux and see the Mississippi. You could put your hands on the towering columns at the edge of the porch and feel the trapped warmth of the late-afternoon Louisiana sun. Tennyson walked toward the window and the free air that was on the other side of the glass.

"Stop right there," cried Aunt Henrietta. "You are forbidden from going on that porch. It's under construction." She pushed open another door to a room that apparently wasn't under construction.

"This is where you'll sleep," she said as the girls went inside, wary as colts. "Zulma will come up to get you settled while I talk to your uncle Twigs about what to do with you."

"Who's Uncle Twigs?" asked Hattie. But Aunt Henrietta had already closed the door with its strange upside-down lock and sealed them inside.

Hattie and Tennyson looked at each other. And then Tennyson said:

"Uncle *Twigs*."

Hattie began to giggle and so did Tennyson. And then they started to laugh. It felt odd to be laughing while they were so upset and confused, but they couldn't help it. They laughed so hard that they didn't notice that the room got a little bit lighter and the vines across the window seemed to recede a little bit.

It suddenly felt like they'd opened a window even though they hadn't.

✦✦✦

Once their laughter had simmered back down, the girls looked around Louvenia's room, whoever she was. This Louvenia slept in a tall bed made of shiny wood, with four posts that nearly touched the ceiling. The mattress was raised so high off the ground that Hattie could barely see over the top of it. Mirrored doors hung lankly from an enormous bureau in the corner, and besides this furniture and the dirt and plaster dust on the floor, the room was empty.

"Help me up onto the bed," Hattie said to Tennyson. She began to climb up as Tennyson shoved her behind. With an "oooph," Hattie went over the top and disappeared into the bed. A cloud of dust swirled up into the air.

"This mattress is *crunchy*," said Hattie from somewhere on top of it.

The door to the room swung open and a new woman barreled in with the girls' duffel bag and gasped,

"God Almighty—get down from there! You think I want to have to make that bed all over again?"

Tennyson froze. Hattie's head appeared over the top of the crunchy mattress. The woman marched up to the bed, seized the foot of the mattress, and yanked it up and down, tossing Hattie around like a rag doll. Hattie leaped down.

The woman put her hands on her hips. She was the skinniest person Hattie and Tennyson had ever seen. Her wrist bones and finger joints and elbows were like knobs and her cheekbones like shields.

"Look at you," said the woman. "Just like little piglets in a pen."

"Are you Zulma?" asked Hattie. "The woman who fell through the stairs last week?"

"Yes, I am, and I would hardly believe that you were Miz Henrietta's nieces if she hadn't told me herself." She went out of the room and came back with a bucket of water, some rags, and a bundle of netting.

"Wash yourselves off," she said. "Start at the top and don't stop till you get to the bottom. And I mean *scrub*—none of this dainty pattin' down."

Tennyson studied the woman. Zulma could have been thirty or she could have been eighty. Her skin was the deepest, richest chocolate, her dress the color of raspberries in August, and her apron buttercup yellow. It was a shock to see such rich colors inside a colorless ice temple like Aigredoux, and Tennyson wondered how those colors didn't melt the house down.

"First I have a question," said Hattie. "Why is the bed crunchy?"

" 'Cause it's stuffed with the moss you see hangin' from the trees," Zulma said. "Don't bother puttin' those dresses back on. I bet Miz Henrietta is gonna burn 'em up."

This was too much, even for Tennyson.

"Then what are we supposed to wear?" she exclaimed.

"Your aunt's gettin' you some clothes from the attic," Zulma said. "Now march over to that bucket while I put the net up."

She unraveled the netting and threw it over the tops of the bedposts, casting a filmy tent over the bed.

"Is that for the 'squitoes?" asked Hattie, wiggling out of her dress. "We don't need one. 'Squitoes don't like us. Mama said we got bit so much when we were little that they got tired of us and now they leave us alone."

"This ain't for mosquitoes," said Zulma, tugging the netting this way and that. "It's to keep you from gettin' smothered by the ceiling."

"What?" said the girls.

"All that ceiling plaster's fallin' down," Zulma said. "Do you want to wake up lookin' like you fell into the flour barrel?"

"I suppose not," conceded Hattie, dipping a frayed cloth into the water bucket. "Zulma, why are all of the locks upside down?"

"Don't you know anything? When a lock's upside down, it confuses any bad ghosts who might want to let themselves in."

"Oh," said Hattie.

Tennyson scrubbed Hattie and soon Hattie stopped looking

like a pink and brown tabby cat. Then Tennyson washed herself. The water was as warm as the air and didn't make her feel any cleaner.

"Get those feet done too," Zulma said, but no matter how hard the girls scrubbed, the bottoms of their feet stayed the color of the dirt on the forest floor around Innisfree.

Aunt Henrietta swished in, handed Zulma a pile of attic clothes, and left again without saying a word.

"Wear these fancy ones," Zulma told them, shaking out two worn dresses. "You're eatin' dinner in the dining room tonight."

"Whose dresses are these?" asked Hattie, putting one on. It was so long that the bottom gathered in a cloth puddle around her feet. The old matted lace on the shoulders and wrists swayed like cobwebs.

"They belonged to Miz Henrietta when she was round your age," Zulma said. "And the good Lord only knows how old they were then. They might've even been Miz Louvenia's."

"Zulma!" called Aunt Henrietta from downstairs.

"It never stops round here," said Zulma, rolling her eyes and taking the water bucket. As she walked out through the tall door, she looked back at Hattie and Tennyson and shook her head.

"Look at the both of you," she said. "You could be ghosts, little Fontaines from the old days. As if the past don't haunt this house enough already."

And she closed the door.

Chapter Four
THE DINNER PARTY

The room turned orange and then gray as the sun set. Tennyson and Hattie slid the window up and tried to push the shutters open, but vines held them in place. As Tennyson pushed, the damp seam on the back of her dress ripped open, revealing her smooth brown back.

A bell rang downstairs. A minute later, it rang again. Then came footsteps, up the wood stairs and the marble ones and down the hallway past the rooms that were under construction.

"What're you waitin' for, an escort?" huffed Zulma. "That's the dinner bell. You're keepin' Miz Henrietta and Mister Thomas waitin' on your first night at Aigredoux."

She carried an oil lamp. The light and shadows bounced

around on the walls as Tennyson and Hattie followed Zulma down the grand staircase.

Aunt Henrietta must have had a bucket of water in her room too, because the plaster from the vine fight on the front porch was all washed off. Her dress was the sort of thing worn by the women on the walls of the Hall of Ancestors.

"This is my husband," she said, gesturing toward a man seated at the far end of a long, long table. It seemed as long as the smashed-shell driveway outside. "He is also your uncle Thomas. He is known by friends and relations as Uncle Twigs, but you may not call him that until you are better acquainted."

Uncle Twigs stood up and bowed slightly. He was tall and terribly white, like a glass of milk, and he wore what had once been fine pale linen breeches. An ivory cane propped him up.

Aunt Henrietta sat down at the other end of the table. Halfway down the table were two place settings for the girls, across from each other. Beeswax candles burned in the wall sconces and in candelabras on the table.

An empty place setting shone on the table next to Uncle Twigs.

"Is that for Zulma?" asked Hattie, looking around for the woman. "Where'd she go?"

"Zulma eats in the kitchen, after she's served our dinner," Aunt Henrietta said. "Genteel Southerners always set an extra place, in case a visitor comes."

Hattie looked confused. "If the plate's just going to go empty, I don't see why Zulma doesn't sit there."

"Be quiet!" Aunt Henrietta commanded. "Zulma is a *servant*. And I do not want to have to remind you again that you may not speak unless I or Uncle Twigs addresses you."

"That's *quite* incorrect," shouted Uncle Twigs from a mile away. "It sounds much better if you say 'Uncle Twigs or I.' "

"It sounded fine the way I said it," said Aunt Henrietta.

"No, it sounded *quite* ill educated," Uncle Twigs called. He produced a book from under the table, fixed a monocle to his left eye, licked his right index finger, and flicked through the pages. "Aha—there, you see. You should always use *I* in the second position in that sentence sequence—it says so right there on page twenty-seven."

"What is that book?" asked Hattie.

"It is none other than the most authoritative grammar manual of the English language," shouted Uncle Twigs, his monocle glinting in the candlelight. "In case you didn't know, I am the president of the Louisiana Society for the Strict Enforcement of the Proper Use of the English Language. I keep a dictionary and thesaurus right here as well, on a shelf on the underside of this table. Did you know that the majority of grammatical atrocities are committed at dining events? This way I am always prepared."

"Oh," said Hattie.

"I told you that you may *not* speak at the table!" cried Aunt Henrietta.

A hinged door swung open and Zulma carried in a tray of soup bowls.

"Thank you, Zulma," Aunt Henrietta sang out. "And what do we have tonight?"

"Potato," said Zulma, setting down the bowls with a clatter. "Like we had last night, and the night before, and every night for the last ten years," and she disappeared back through the swinging door.

Wax splattered from the candles onto the table. Tennyson looked around, paying particular attention to the two portraits above the fireplace. One was a man and one was a woman.

Aunt Henrietta saw Tennyson looking at the portraits.

"Do you know who those people are?" she asked.

"No," answered Tennyson.

"That is none other than Atlas Fontaine and his wife, Julia Bessinou Fontaine," declared Aunt Henrietta, drawing blank stares from Hattie and Tennyson. "Of the New Orleans Bessinous," she added, clearly waiting for recognition from the girls, with which she was not rewarded.

"Not to be confused with the Atlanta Bessinous," Uncle Twigs informed them. "They were *quite* ill bred. Descended from hatmakers and pig farmers, although they'd never admit to it."

Hattie giggled.

"Oh, for heaven's sake," Aunt Henrietta said impatiently. "The people in these portraits are your great-great-great-great-grandparents, and they built Aigredoux, which was only one of their five plantations. And they are the founders of the Fontaine dynasty. Which, incidentally, ends with the two of you. You girls are the heiresses of Aigredoux."

This pronouncement drew more blank stares from the girls. Not knowing what else to do, Hattie picked up her soup bowl and started to drink from it.

"What in God's name are you doing?" Aunt Henrietta cried. "Use your spoon! Where are your table manners?"

"We don't have a table at Innisfree," Hattie said.

"No table!" Aunt Henrietta gasped. "You really *have* been living like savages."

She put down her spoon in alarm.

"*Something* must be done," she exclaimed. "And right away, before you're both completely ruined. Although it may be too late already."

"What do you mean, before we're ruined?" asked Hattie.

"Well, you barely resemble *girls*, much less ladies," said Aunt Henrietta. "I have a nearly impossible task before me. But regardless, I am going to take charge of your education. We'll start lessons later this week."

"This soup is *quite* thin, wouldn't you say?" added Uncle Twigs. "Let's ask Zulma for turtle and sherry soup tomorrow night."

"We ain't got any turtles and we ain't got any sherry," said Zulma as she set down a rather scrawny cooked chicken in front of Uncle Twigs.

"I certainly do love a bit of turtle and sherry soup now and then," he said wistfully, and sawed the chicken into pieces.

Aunt Henrietta was still staring at Hattie and Tennyson, with a strange look on her face. "It's happened at last," she said ominously. "Fate has once again concerned itself with the destiny of the Fontaines. You have been returned to Aigredoux for a reason."

Suddenly a piercing scream came from outside, as though a lady had been stabbed on the front porch. Hattie and Tennyson shot up from the table. But Aunt Henrietta and Uncle Twigs remained seated, and Zulma calmly distributed the meager chicken parts.

"Oh, that's just Bondurant," shouted Uncle Twigs. "Don't mind him."

"Him?" said Hattie. "But it sounded like a woman!" The girls sat warily back down at the table.

"I hate that peacock," Zulma said. "He just waits till you sit down at the dinner table—or till you're closin' your eyes in bed—and then screams like a demon."

"Peacocks are sacred in no less than thirty-seven cultures," Uncle Twigs advised no one in particular.

"Just let me get my hands on him, and I'll show you what a sacred Thanksgiving dinner looks like," Zulma muttered as she swung back through the door.

Aunt Henrietta ignored the measly chicken legs on her plate.

"Tell me what your father has told you about our family," she said to Tennyson.

Tennyson didn't know what to say. Her hand went instinctively to the torn seam in the back of her dress, closing it up against Aunt Henrietta's strange stare.

"Our father never talks about you," she answered.

"Well, never mind what he says about *me* in particular," pressed Aunt Henrietta. "But what has he told you about the Fontaines?"

"Mama told us that the Fontaines were rich once, but they lost all of their money after the big war," Hattie said carelessly, licking her soup spoon.

Tennyson kicked at her sister, but the table was too wide to reach her. Hattie went on.

"She says that all of the money was made from slaves, and because of that Aigredoux deserved to be painted blood-red. Which is why we were surprised that it wasn't any color at all, like—"

"Enough!" cried Aunt Henrietta, standing up. "Leave at once! Go to bed—both of you! From now on, you'll eat in the kitchen, until you learn how to behave decently."

The painted eyes of Atlas Fontaine and his wife, Julia, followed the girls as they ran out of the dining room. Then the eyes of the painted Fontaines hanging in the Hall of Ancestors followed them as they went up the grand staircase. Tennyson felt their stares on her bare back until she and Hattie were safely in their room with the door closed.

Or Louvenia's room, rather. Whoever she was.

✳✳✳

Tennyson peered through a crack in the shutters. The world outside had turned blue in the moonlight. Like the front lawn, gnarled trees and hungry vines filled the backyard. In the middle of this mess of vines and roots and dry grass stood a small village of buildings. One of them had probably been a chicken shack or a washhouse, perhaps a stable. Maybe one of them had been a kitchen.

In any case, you couldn't tell what those buildings had been, for they had all been slowly melting like butter into the ground, their soggy wooden walls bending, groaning, and sighing as they decomposed, year after year. Some of them had disappeared altogether, leaving only their chimneys jutting up like tombstones from the ground.

Hattie was crying again.

"Aunt Henrietta is hateful," she said.

"Go to sleep," Tennyson told her. "Things always seem worse at night."

"I want Mama to come back," Hattie said.

"She will," said Tennyson, feeling guilty, like she was telling a lie. "She probably just needed some time alone to work on her stories and her poems."

"She didn't have to go away," whimpered Hattie. "I would have left her alone. We could have played hide-and-seek for days so she could have the house to herself."

Tennyson pulled aside the net shrouding the bed and helped

Hattie up onto the ghost-moss mattress. She petted Hattie's hair until the girl's breathing was deep and regular.

Then Tennyson rummaged around in their duffel bag on the floor, digging down deep, under the tangle of threadbare dresses and the underpants and Hattie's stuffed elephant that had been loved so much that it no longer resembled an elephant at all. At the bottom of the bag were things that had belonged to their mother.

A pair of white satin shoes that Sadie had worn to a cotillion dance in New Orleans, before she and Emery had run away to Innisfree to play house. Several tattered issues of the *Sophisticate.* And at the very bottom, Tennyson found what she was looking for: Sadie's fountain pen.

Now she needed paper.

Tennyson pushed back the huge mirrored doors of the bureau in the corner. Inside hung several more old dresses, and on the bottom sat a dusty stack of papers, tied with a now-gray silk ribbon. Music was printed on these papers, but the backs of the pages were blank.

On the first page were the words:

Music for the Harp & Soul

Tennyson smirked at the corny title.

She lay on her stomach on the floor and began to write on the backs of the music sheets. She wrote about their journey in the truck and Zulma and the rage of Aunt Henrietta and

Bondurant and the huge dying temple that towered to the sky and creaked around them. When she was done, Tennyson propped these paper stories up against the walls so Hattie would wake up the next day and feel like she was back at Innisfree. Like she was in the main room with the rope hanging from the rafter, filled with their mother's words.

Then she climbed onto the bed herself and wondered where Sadie and Emery were sleeping that night, if they were together or still many worlds apart.

Chapter Five

LOUVENIA

Tennyson usually slept on her stomach, like a baby. She always had. And she could sleep through practically anything. A thunderstorm. A flood. A noisy fight.

But tonight as Tennyson lay on her stomach, the moss in the mattress formed into sticks and poked into her limbs and scratched at her face. Her baby-like sleep fought back against the moss, because Tennyson was eager to dream warm dreams and not be awake in a strange room that overlooked a blue landscape of broken buildings. She pushed against the mattress, and it rewarded her by hardening under her body. Angry now, Tennyson opened her eyes.

Hattie was gone. Tennyson felt around the bed for her sister and found that she herself wasn't in the moss bed at all. Her hands grasped tree roots and she realized that she was curled up by one of the gnarled trees in the oak alley outside.

It was just before dawn. Tennyson could tell because grayness had replaced the cold moonlight, the sort of gray that catches fire when the sun comes up and then relaxes into pink and yellow daylight. The vines had receded from the driveway and the smashed shells shone like dull pearls.

She had never walked in her sleep before. No one at Innisfree ever walked in their sleep—not even Sadie, who was so restless that her hands always trembled.

Suddenly a barefooted man padded right past her, a stranger. He wore threadbare field clothes and his skin was the color of black ink. About ten feet away, he stopped and slowly turned around and around, staring up at the tree branches. In his hands was a shiny red lacquer box.

Another man walked by carrying a shiny red lacquer box, and then came another man, and another. Soon the hazy outlines of twenty barefooted men were there with red boxes, and they placed these boxes at the roots of each tree in the tunnel. Tennyson stared at them, not moving.

The first man knelt over his box. Then, with a shout, he tore off the top of it and dozens of huge spiders ran out and skittered toward Tennyson. She leaped up and screamed, stubbing her toes as she stumbled over the tree roots. The spiders raced past her and crawled right up the trunk of the tree and out onto all of the branches. Then all of the other men opened their red boxes too and soon there were so many spiders on all of the trees in the alley that it looked like their bark was moving.

Usually Hattie was the one who asked the questions, but since she was all alone, Tennyson had to ask them for herself.

"Why are you letting spiders up into the trees?" she shouted to the men. "And why do they live in those shiny red boxes?"

They ignored her. So she tried again.

"How did those spiders get so big?"

No response.

This must be a dream, Tennyson thought. *They're not answering because they can't see me and they can't hear me.* She let out a little shriek, just because she could. No one paid any attention to her. Tennyson was a dream ghost. Her heart beat faster. For a second she felt gleeful and free, like she was getting away with something sneaky.

The spiders in the trees began to weave great webs in the branches. They worked faster and faster and soon the air between every branch and trunk turned into spider silk, as though a vast fine cloth the color of air had been draped over the entire oak alley. Then there was the crunch of footsteps and more men came. These men carried fireplace bellows and they walked up and down the tree alley, blowing gold dust from the bellows onto the great sticky webs.

Suddenly the early-morning gray light caught on fire as the dawn sun burst over the horizon, and Tennyson was nearly blinded by the searing glint of gold on the webs. It was such a sight that for a minute you had to wonder if God was coming.

In fact, the beauty overwhelmed Tennyson so much that she had to turn away. And when she turned her back on the sharp blazing gold, Tennyson expected to find relief, but she didn't. The other direction turned out to be sharp too, but instead of blazing gold there was a great blaze of white.

That white blaze was Aigredoux, basking in the flame of dawn sunlight, restored to its former glory.

It wasn't until she saw Aigredoux like this, blinding and beautiful and powerful, that Tennyson truly understood what it meant to be a Fontaine.

***

A cry came from the river:

"The boats are here!"

All of the men rushed down the smashed-shell driveway toward the river. In this dream there was no levee and the deadly silver currents of the Mississippi shone under the sun. An armada of boats choked the river around Aigredoux's docks. One man would call out what was about to be unloaded, and the men would go to work.

The first shout:

"Swans!"

White feathers swirled into the air as crates of swans were handed off the boats and doves too. The swans bucked and snapped their beaks until the men released them into a pond by the house. The doves cooed as they were put into towering wicker cages shaped like castles, forts, churches, and pagodas, and soon these little houses made an eccentric kingdom across the vast front lawns.

The foreman's next call:

"Chandeliers!"

Then there was the sound of tinkling glass, and fifty crystal chandeliers trembled and glinted as they were carried off one of the barges. The men hung these chandeliers from low tree branches around Aigredoux, where they swung gently in the breeze and cast rainbows across the grass.

The parade was only just beginning and now came food. First came food from trees: green-orange papayas and mangoes, yellow bananas, even coconuts. A pineapple fell out of a box and landed at Tennyson's feet. Then came the food from the sea.

"Oysters!"

Indeed, great ice tubs of oysters, crawdads, shrimp, and clams. All of this was followed by ice tubs of champagne, and all of that ice steamed up in the daytime heat, cooling the breeze as the tubs were carried up through the gold tunnel.

Then a huge black lacquer box emerged on the decks of one of the boats. All of the workers backed away from it and looked up at the foreman, who just stared at the box and rubbed his chin in puzzlement.

"I don't know what's in there," he said finally.

No one did. A decision was made to open it up. The men drew straws and the unlucky ones were handed crowbars. Tennyson's heart pounded as the men began to pry off the lid. At last with a creak and a *pop* the lid flew off and into the air burst thousands of gold and red butterflies.

Looking relieved, the foreman called out:

"Flowers!"

And then a hundred enormous bouquets of flowers emerged from the boats, their vases so big that you couldn't wrap your arms all the way around them. This moving garden teetered and swayed as the men carried it up through the gold tunnel and into the house.

I'm going to follow them inside, Tennyson thought. *No one can see me anyway. I'm a dream ghost.*

She ran up to the front stairs of the house and looked up at Aigredoux, half expecting it to disappear like a mirage. Wide marble stairs led up to the front porch and marble statues of Greek gods guarded the entranceway. Flowers spilled from window boxes and long garlands of jasmine and magnolias coursed down the tall columns. Tennyson put her foot on the first step.

It was not a mirage. The cool marble stairs did not disappear. The towering blinding-white columns and the marble gods did not disappear.

So she walked up the stairs and through the front door.

❖❖❖

Light flooded the inside of the house and people flooded it too, mostly rushing servant women wearing black clothes and white aprons.

"A perfect day for a wedding!" boomed a voice from the top of the grand marble stairway.

Tennyson looked up at the man with the booming voice and recognized him at once. He was Atlas Fontaine, her ancestor, and he looked just like his portrait above the fireplace in the dining room. His hair was curly like Emery's and his face showed that he was someone who truly loved pleasure.

"Where is my wife?" he called, bending over the banister. "I want my beautiful wife to come out from the parlor and kiss me."

Heels clicked on marble behind Tennyson and a hard voice said,

"Stop making a fool of yourself in front of the servants, Atlas."

Tennyson turned around. She wasn't usually scared of people, but she was scared of this woman. Then she remembered the other portrait above the dining room fireplace and saw that this woman was her great-great-great-great-grandmother, Julia Bessinou Fontaine.

"Doesn't it all look wonderful?" Atlas said, coming down the stairs.

"It all looks expensive," said Julia, looking out the front door at the commotion. A scarlet butterfly flew into the hallway.

"Good," said Atlas, reaching his wife and kissing her on the cheek. "Because it was. I wanted this to be a celebration unlike any other. Even the emperors of Rome would be jealous! Louisiana will remember the wedding of Louvenia Fontaine for a hundred years."

Louvenia! thought Tennyson. The mysterious Louvenia, whose room she and Hattie lived in. Whose crunchy moss bed

Hattie was sleeping in at this very moment—and Tennyson herself, presumably.

"Just one thing, missy," Atlas went on, playfully grabbing Julia's wrist. "When our guests arrive, don't go telling them that this was all *your* idea! This was my vision, through and through—and I won't have you taking credit for it."

Julia's expression softened. "I wouldn't dream of it," she said, putting her hand over Atlas's.

"Now, where's the bride?" Atlas asked.

"She's in the parl—"

A beastly scream rang out from the ladies' parlor:

"Mooooottttttttthhhhhhher!"

One of the servants dropped a tray of linen napkins on the marble floor.

"She's in the parlor," Julia said lightly. "They're putting the finishing touches on the wedding portrait. I'll be right back."

Tennyson followed Julia into the parlor, and there stood Louvenia Fontaine, swathed in a white silk wedding dress that billowed and spread across the room. Yards of lace wreathed her head and cascaded down to the floor. Diamonds glistened at her throat and on her wrists, and a peacock sat at her feet. A young servant girl fanned her with a big palm frond, and across the room stood a man behind a huge canvas, amidst an explosion of paintbrushes and paint tubes.

"Mother, make that simpleton finish the painting already," Louvenia yelled, pointing at the artist.

"Stop shouting, Louvenia," said Julia. "It's unladylike."

"I don't have to be a lady. We're rich enough that I can behave however I want."

Tennyson crept into the room to get a closer look at Louvenia. She accidentally stepped on the peacock's tail feathers and the bird let out a horrible scream.

"Get out of here, you horrid animal," cried Louvenia, kicking it through her wedding dress. The peacock ran out into the hallway, squawking.

How could it feel me? wondered Tennyson. She guessed that animals could sense dream ghosts, just like they could sense real ones.

"What set that bird off like that?" asked Julia, looking around.

"Who cares," said Louvenia, swatting away the palm frond. "If you hit me with that one more time—" she said to the servant girl, clenching her fist.

"Louvenia, hold still!" commanded Julia. "This is your wedding portrait, for heaven's sake. He's almost finished. Be patient."

"I don't want to be patient. I want to be finished. If he doesn't finish, I'm going to make myself faint."

"Don't you dare!"

"I'm going to," Louvenia promised, and held her breath. Then she fell like an axed oak, facedown into a cushion of silk and lace.

Julia sighed.

"Help me put her on the fainting couch," she said to the servant girl. "And don't touch her dress."

They carried Louvenia by her wrists and ankles over to a funny couch, one side of which was much lower than the other, like a slide or a chute. They plopped the bride-to-be on top of it, with her head on the down side and her feet in the air.

"That way the blood all goes down to her head," Julia explained to the artist. "She'll come to in a minute."

"This happens every single time I paint a portrait of her," cried the artist. "I cannot work like this." He threw down his paintbrush and left the room.

Julia crossed her arms and stared down at her daughter.

"Wake up, Louvenia. I have diamond earrings for you."

Louvenia automatically opened her eyes and sat straight up, her hand out.

"Is Laurent here yet?" she asked.

"Not yet," said Julia. "He'll be here at any moment."

Louvenia affixed the diamonds to her ears. "Mother, do you think that Laurent's a good match for me?" she asked. "Is he really good enough to be my husband?"

"He's a Bossier," said Julia. "So he's a perfect match for a Fontaine. You're both from the greatest families in Louisiana. Of course, I'm not fond of his temper, and I don't particularly approve of the way he duels at the drop of a hat. But you can't have everything."

"He'd better not be late," said Louvenia darkly. "He's always fashionably late to everything."

Tennyson thought that she'd be late too if she were facing marriage to someone like Louvenia. In fact, she couldn't wait to get away from her relative, and she ran back outside to see what was happening with Atlas's celebration.

Long silk-covered banquet tables now lined the lawns and servants were laying solid-gold plates and crystal glasses on top. Peacocks strutted across the lawns.

"Effie, hurry up and bring out more plates!" shouted one of the women setting the tables. She turned to another servant. "Where is that girl?"

"Didn't you hear?" Another woman frowned.

"Hear what?"

"Have you been livin' under a rock or something? Last week, Miz Julia sold Effie's husband. And that very night Effie tried to run away after him. But they caught her and the overseer whipped her senseless and she's *still* in bed. She can't even roll over."

Tennyson froze, and suddenly she realized.

All of these servants weren't merely servants.

They were slaves.

They were the reason that Emery and Sadie hated Aigredoux and wanted it to be colored blood-red.

The gold webs and the peacocks and glinting chandeliers made Tennyson feel sick all of a sudden. She'd been tricked into devouring the candy of Aigredoux, the kind that stays in your blood, and she wanted to throw it up. The bustle around her went on, but she didn't hear or see a thing. She ran down the front stairs and huddled behind one of the statues, pulling her knees to her chest and closing her eyes.

When I open my eyes, I'll be back in bed, she told herself. *On the count of three.*

One.

Two.

Three.

But when Tennyson opened her eyes, she was still there in the shadow of the marble gods.

She couldn't leave the dream until it was ready to let her go.

❖❖❖

Then it was late afternoon and the guests began to arrive.

A line of horse-drawn carriages stretched all the way down to the river. A grand orchestra had assembled on the lawn and the musicians tuned their instruments.

Atlas and Julia stood on the front porch to meet their guests and next to them stood four young men. Tennyson crept up the stairs and stood behind them. There was an endless swirl of dresses and perfumes and swords and colognes as the guests climbed the front stairs to greet their hosts.

Soon a man in a military uniform climbed the stairs and a brief hush fell over the crowd as it parted for him.

"Major General," called Atlas. "This is an honor."

"Congratulations," said the major general. "A fine day and a fine match."

"This is my wife, Julia," Atlas said. "And please meet my sons." The four young men stepped forward. "This is John, Langdon, Thomas, and young Henry."

"All fighting age, I see," said the major general.

"Not this one," said Langdon, grabbing Henry by the ear. "He's still in diapers."

"Cut it out," shrieked Henry, slapping at his brother's hand.

The major general smiled. "I look forward to seeing all of you brave lads in my army when the war starts."

Julia's face turned stony. "The war hasn't started yet," she said. "And if you have any sense, you won't start one. Some of us have money to make."

"Julia!" cried Atlas. "Please don't mind her, Major General. The preparations for the wedding have been most overwhelming. Enjoy the party."

Just then, a voice hissed from the front door:

"Mother!"

"Louvenia!" said Julia. "Go back inside. No one must see you in your dress."

"Is he here yet?"

"Who?"

"What do you mean, who? Laurent! My fiancé!"

"Not yet," said Julia, shoving her inside and closing the door. "Be patient!"

But soon the line of carriages thinned and the lawns were filled with nearly a thousand people and Louvenia's fiancé still did not come. The sun began to sink behind the house.

"Play something!" Julia said to the orchestra, which started a cheery waltz. But soon the guests grew restless and everyone wondered what was going on.

"Should we begin the dinner, ma'am?" asked one of the slaves. "All the food's ready. It'll go bad if we don't serve it up soon."

"All right," Julia said reluctantly. "Just the first four courses. And have the men light the torches in the oak alley," even though the torches weren't supposed to be lit until Louvenia and Laurent walked down the alley during their wedding ceremony. "I'm going to wring that boy's neck," she whispered to Atlas.

"I'm sure there's an explanation," Atlas whispered back, wearing a tight smile for his guests.

A boat drew up to the dock, and a man got out and ran up the alley toward the house.

"Who is that?" Julia asked, squinting in the hazy dusk light.

"It's Tom Granier," said Atlas. "Laurent's best man."

All of the guests turned from their oysters and champagne to watch what would happen.

"Mr. Atlas," said Tom, staggering breathlessly up the steps. "Mrs. Julia."

"What's happening?" hissed Julia. "Where is Laurent?"

Tom looked up at them and Tennyson could see terror in his eyes. "He's on the boat," he said.

Julia drew up to her full height. "Oh, I see," she thundered. "What, is he too drunk to get off? I'll horsewhip him!"

"He's not drunk," said Tom.

"Then what?"

Tears spilled down Tom's cheeks. "There was a duel this morning in New Orleans," he said. "And Laurent didn't win."

A gasp went up from the crowd of guests, who all got up and ran to the oak alley. They stood behind the torchlit gold webs and watched in horror as four men walked slowly up the alley to the house.

On their shoulders they carried a coffin.

Julia's hand went to her throat.

"God in heaven," she cried. She turned to her sons. "Run inside. Do *not* let your sister come out. And don't tell her anything—not yet."

But then they heard footsteps creak on the balcony above their heads and they knew it was too late. There stood Louvenia in her sea of silk and lace, and when she saw her groom she let out a terrible scream and sank to her knees.

And with the sound of that scream ringing in her ears, Tennyson woke up.

Chapter Six

THE BONE FORESTS

"Tennyson," Hattie whispered. "Tennyson—did you hear that?"

"But I was dreaming," said Tennyson, still groggy with sleep. "How could you have heard the scream too?" Her sweaty hair stuck to her neck and back. The sun had only just risen and already the room was hot. A fine shower of plaster had fallen from the ceiling in the night, dusting the floor and the mosquito net.

"What are you talking about?" cried Hattie. "That came from right outside, from the trees!"

Another scream pierced the air and Hattie buried her damp face in Tennyson's stomach.

"I know what it is," Tennyson said, awake now, and she marched over to the window and shoved the shutters open.

There on a tree branch sat Bondurant, his blue and green and black silken feathers shimmering dully in the dawn light. Tennyson had never seen a peacock, or any bird, for that matter, look *smug* before. But then again, they were at Aigredoux, where everything had to be peculiar.

"Go away!" she hissed at Bondurant. The bird blinked at her and didn't move a muscle. Tennyson wadded up one of the papers on the floor and threw it at him, hitting him right between the eyes. "Get out of here!"

Bondurant opened his beak and let out one last shrill screech, just to remind Tennyson who was boss. And then he tottered back up the branch.

"Tennyson!" cried Hattie. "Look! The shutters opened! What happened to the vines? We couldn't budge them at all yesterday."

Tennyson stared at the window in surprise. The vines had indeed shrunk back from the window.

"And look!" exclaimed Hattie, leaping up and down and clapping. "The papers! Just like at home! What's on them?" She slid off the bed.

"Some stories I wrote last night," said Tennyson. "They're good too."

"What're they about?"

"Our trip here," said Tennyson. "Our family. Everything. And I have more to write about today." She told Hattie about her dream.

"I wonder if all that stuff really happened," said Hattie, listening intently.

"I doubt it," said Tennyson. "It was just a dream."

"But why did you dream it?" Hattie pressed. "You never had a dream like that at Innisfree."

"I don't know."

The soothing clink of dishes came from downstairs.

"Breakfast," cried Hattie, forgetting the strange dream as the girls ran through Aigredoux's rotten dark halls to a makeshift kitchen in the back of the house. Zulma was there in her raspberry red dress and bright yellow apron, cooking a big pot of grits. Coffee hiccuped out of a pot onto the stove.

"Oh, you still here?" she said when the girls came into the room. "You're hungry, I suppose."

Hattie nodded. "Aunt Henrietta sent us to bed during dinner last night," she said. "We're starving."

"Well, there ain't nothin' fancy to eat," said Zulma. "Just grits."

"I hate grits," said Hattie.

"Then go hungry," said Zulma.

The girls ate grits.

"I wish we had some of that fancy wedding food," said Hattie to Tennyson. "Zulma, listen to what Tennyson dreamed last night. There was a wedding here with all these gold-covered spiderwebs and oysters and then it all turned into a funeral instead."

Zulma turned around and looked from Hattie to Tennyson. "You dreamed *what*?" she asked Tennyson.

It was not a friendly question. Tennyson's guard went up.

"I had a dream about Louvenia getting married, that's all," she said.

"Tell her about the black box of butterflies," Hattie exclaimed, her mouth full. "And the boats, and Effie the slave—"

"You didn't just *dream* about all that," Zulma interrupted, her hands on her hips. "Your father's been tellin' you family stories."

"Our father never talks about Aigredoux," said Tennyson. "We didn't even know who Aunt Henrietta was before we got here."

"Then you're dreamin' real things," Zulma said, backing up slowly. "That wedding, it really happened. With all the spiderwebs and the funeral and all. It's like you're doin' voodoo or somethin'. Makes the hair stand right up on my arms." She narrowed her eyes at Tennyson. "Either that or you're lyin' to me. Which is it? Voodoo or lies?"

Tennyson didn't know how to answer this. "I'm not lying," she said at last.

Zulma eyed Tennyson suspiciously as she took the breakfast bowls away from the girls and dropped them into a basin of water.

"We're goin' out," she said.

"Where?" asked Hattie.

"To the post office, to mail Miz Henrietta's letters," said Zulma. "I'm showin' you the way so you can do it next time. Now that you're here, you gotta do something to earn your keep."

"Can I have some coffee?" Hattie asked.

"A child drinkin' coffee!" whooped Zulma. "I never heard of such a thing! Go wash your face and meet me at the front door."

Hattie looked confused as she walked out of the room. "Our mother lets us drink coffee every morning," she said.

Tennyson started after her—but Zulma grabbed her arm.

"Now listen to me, voodoo girl," she said in a low voice. "I don't know what you're up to, but I'm gonna be watchin' you. And don't you pester Miz Henrietta with your dream nonsense either. Keep your lip buttoned—hear me?"

Tennyson just stared at her.

"I mean it," Zulma told her.

And just like that, a battle began and lines were drawn in the sand. It wasn't clear yet what the fight was about. But Tennyson suddenly knew that she was in it on her own.

❖❖❖

So many letters needed mailing that Zulma, Hattie, and Tennyson each had to carry a stack.

"Aunt Henrietta must have a lot of friends," said Hattie as they walked through the tree tunnel in front of the house. It had rained in the night and steam rose from the ground in the morning heat, swirling around their feet and erasing all hard edges around them.

"These ain't letters to her friends," Zulma told them. "They're goin' to the government of the United States of America."

"What?" asked Hattie, stumbling along in the vines. "Why is she writing to the government?"

"She's been writin' dozens of letters every week for as long as I can remember," said Zulma. "And 'fore that, her mother sent letters, and 'fore *that,* her mother's mother sent letters. Tryin' to get the government to pay back the Fontaine fortune it took durin' the big war. You know, the war between the states."

Tennyson looked down at her aunt's curvy, feminine handwriting. The letters looked like tea invitations, not letters to officials in Washington, D.C.

"The government stole our family's money?" Hattie asked. "Is that why we're poor and Aigredoux's falling down?"

"It's a long story, and I don't feel like tellin' it," said Zulma, forging ahead.

"How would she get it back now anyway?" asked Tennyson. "The Civil War was seventy years ago."

"That doesn't matter," said Zulma. "To Miz Henrietta, it was yesterday. And mailin' her letters is gonna be your job from now on."

The rocky dirt road along the river felt wonderful under Tennyson's bare feet. Even though the air was hot and heavy, it smelled and tasted delicious to her after the dead air of Aigredoux. But soon the road wound out of the lush cane fields and led into a patch of woods that had for some reason decided to die. Instead of turning into dirt, the trees and branches and roots from these woods turned themselves white. They shed all of their bark and the smooth skin underneath bleached itself out in the hot sun. These tree skeletons jutted up from the earth and steam coiled around the blanched roots.

"Hold your breath," Zulma told them. "There're bad spirits

in there who want to steal your breath, and they'll try anything to get it. If you go in there, you'll disappear forever."

"You mean the trees swallow you up, like the river swallows up little girls?" Hattie asked.

"Hold your breath!" said Zulma, taking a deep breath and puffing out her cheeks.

But then when they were done holding their breath and the white bone forest was behind them, there was another bone forest in front of them. These bones looked like enormous trees but they had no branches. Dying vines covered them, hanging down like long tendrils of black hair.

"Those trees are weird," said Hattie. "They're standing in a square."

"They ain't trees," said Zulma. "They're columns from a house that burned down. It was a fine big house like Aigredoux, called Bon Vivant. But one night God threw fire onto it and now the columns are all that's left standin'."

The black hair vines rippled in the breeze.

"Well, that was nice of God to leave the columns, at least," Hattie offered.

"He didn't leave 'em behind so the family who built Bon Vivant had something left," said Zulma. "He left 'em to remind 'em of what could've been."

Tennyson thought that this was a sour way of looking at it, but she kept quiet.

They walked further down the road, which led them back into yet another cane field, and soon they walked past a clearing filled with curious white marble boxes and little white marble houses in neat rows.

"What's in those boxes?" asked Hattie. "And who lives in those tiny houses?"

"Dead people live there," Zulma said. "They're graves."

"Oh," faltered Hattie, reaching for Tennyson's hand. "Why aren't the graves underground?"

"Can't bury anyone in the ground round here," Zulma told her. "We're so far below sea level that the bodies would pop out durin' a rainstorm and start dancin'."

Hattie screamed and her letters scattered everywhere. Zulma smiled and kept walking.

In the distance, a little whitewashed house stood in the cane field, and when they got closer, Tennyson and Hattie saw that it was a house like Innisfree, splintery and cheerful, propped up on stilts. A hand-painted sign nailed to the front proclaimed:

Ascension Parish Post Office

Inside it smelled like apple tobacco. Its single room appeared to be empty but smoke rose like white silk ribbons from behind the high front counter.

"Zipporah Tweed, get up off your behind and take these letters from us," said Zulma.

"I swear, Miz Zulma," said a man's voice from behind the counter. "Your voice is like the music of angels."

"Oh, hush," Zulma said, dumping the letters on the counter

and peering over. "You're the laziest postmaster in all Louisiana. Every time I come in here, you're settin' in front of that window and smokin' that pipe. What're you starin' at all day?"

Zipporah Tweed stood up and blew out a fluffy white cloud. The smoke swirled playfully around his gray beard and the striped railroad cap perched on top of his salt-and-pepper puff of hair.

"I'm starin' at Time passin'," he said benevolently. "Who're these little chickens?"

"They're Mister Emery's daughters," said Zulma.

Zipporah took his pipe out of his mouth and stared at the girls. "Mister Emery!" he exclaimed. "Is he back at Aigredoux? I thought—"

"He ain't back," interrupted Zulma. "His wife went off and left 'em all, and Mister Emery went to find her. So he left the girls with me and Miz Henrietta to look after."

Tennyson suddenly hated Zulma. She hated her for dishing up the story of Sadie's betrayal like cold leftovers, and she stared at the floor so no one would see the hatred in her face.

Silken smoke rose again from Zipporah's pipe and the apple tobacco burned orange as he took a deep drag.

"I swear," he said after a minute.

Tennyson and Hattie piled their letter stacks onto the counter and Zipporah swept them into a big burlap bag with his arm.

"The girls are gonna bring the letters every week from now on," Zulma told him, and she ushered Hattie out the door. But

Tennyson lingered after they left, not wanting to leave the warmth of a kind person and the sweet smell and the window that looked out over Time passing.

Zipporah looked down at her.

"What's your name?"

"Tennyson."

Zipporah whistled. "Now, who went and gave you a name like that?" he asked.

"My mother. She writes poems and stories. Tennyson was a famous poet."

"Oh, I know who Mister Tennyson was all right," Zipporah said, putting down his pipe. He recited:

> "Come away; no more of mirth
>   Is here or merry-making sound.
> The house was builded of the earth,
>   And shall fall again to ground."

"That was one of my mother's favorite poems," said Tennyson. " 'The Deserted House.' How did you know that?"

"I didn't," said Zipporah. "I just always took a shine to it, that's all. Miz Zulma asked what I do all day. There ain't nothin' to do but look out the window—and read. Look here."

Tennyson stood on her toes and peered behind the counter. Dozens of books lay in neat stacks amidst the burlap sacks and letters. Zipporah pulled one out and its gold-lettered title gleamed: *The Poetic Works of Alfred, Lord Tennyson.*

"Hey, voodoo girl," yelled Zulma from outside. "You comin' or not?"

Zipporah looked at Tennyson kindly. "You can come back anytime," he said. "Bet you'll be needin' some time away from Miz Zulma and Miz Henrietta. I'd sure be runnin' out that door every day."

Tennyson allowed herself to smile. Then she and Hattie and Zulma walked back down the river road to Aigredoux, past the skeletons of people and houses and trees that had lived and breathed and mattered a long time ago.

Chapter Seven

LESSONS

"I have called you in here to begin your lessons," Aunt Henrietta told the girls later that afternoon. "This is the ladies' parlor. Across the hallway is the gentlemen's lounge and study, where Uncle Twigs works."

Tennyson and Hattie looked across the front foyer and there behind a big desk sat Uncle Twigs, wearing his monocle, a pale linen suit, and a panama hat. A mosquito net hung down from a beam in the ceiling over the desk. A small chunk of plaster fell from the ceiling and slid down the side of the net.

"You are never to disturb him while he is working," warned Aunt Henrietta. "He has a great many responsibilities as the president of the Louisiana Society for the Strict Enforcement of the Proper Use of the English Language."

"Why's Uncle Twigs sitting under that net?" asked Hattie. "I thought they were only for beds."

"Firstly, you may only address me once I've asked a question which requires your response," said Aunt Henrietta.

"No, that's *quite* incorrect," called Uncle Twigs, without looking up. "Use the word *that* instead of *which*."

Aunt Henrietta ignored him. "Secondly, call him 'Uncle Thomas,'" she went on. "And finally, the net is there because the gentlemen's parlor happens to have a mosquito problem."

Another plaster chunk fell from the ceiling onto the net.

"Ri-i-i-i-ight," said Hattie. "A mosquito problem."

Aunt Henrietta slid the door shut. The whole room was filled with hard, uncomfortable furniture that made you sit very upright. In the corner stood a harp, its strings interlaced with cobwebs and dust. *Music for the Harp and Soul*, Tennyson thought.

"Tell me about your schooling at home," Aunt Henrietta said. "Presumably it has been rather scant. Restricted to starting a fire with two sticks and that sort of thing."

Tennyson grew indignant. "Our mother and father taught us how to read and write when we were practically babies," she said.

"My favorite book is *Through the Looking-Glass*," announced Hattie. "And Tennyson's is *War and Peace*. And my favorite poem is 'The Walrus and the Carpenter.' It has one hundred and eight lines and I know all of them. Want to hear?"

"No, I do not," answered Aunt Henrietta. "As I suspected, your parents have seen fit to give you an unattractively masculine education. *War and Peace!* There will be no more of that here. No more reading of subversive books and poems, no more writing–"

"Why?" exclaimed Hattie. "What's wrong with reading and writing?"

"There is nothing more unpleasant than a girl who *knows* too much," said Aunt Henrietta. "Women who read and write too much seem aggressive, and it's extremely off-putting."

"But our mother reads and writes all the time," protested Tennyson.

"My point exactly," said Aunt Henrietta. "Look how *she* turned out. No good can come to a woman who selfishly focuses on a pen and ignores her femininity and family."

"But you write too," Hattie pointed out. "We mailed about a hundred of your letters to Washington, D.C., only this morning."

"Oh, will you please *be quiet*," Aunt Henrietta cried. "Today I am going to begin schooling you in the feminine arts and set you on the right track. In our first lesson you will learn how to make a charming first impression on a suitor."

"What's a suitor?" asked Hattie.

"A gentleman caller," said Aunt Henrietta florally.

"Oh, lordy," said Hattie under her breath.

Aunt Henrietta pointed in the air like an old-fashioned philosopher.

"Always enchant your suitor with clever chatter," she said.

"Never start with something boring about the weather. Say something like, 'Goodness, Mister So-and-so! Why is it that every time you come into the room, I'm reminded of Apollo?' "

"What's a poll-o," asked Hattie, squirming on the hard bench.

"Apollo is the Greek god of the sun," Aunt Henrietta said. "Now, pretend that I am a suitor coming to call, and say something lovely to me." She glided out of the room and stormed back in, wearing what she thought was a very manly look on her face.

Hattie and Tennyson just looked at her.

"Go on, then," hissed Aunt Henrietta. "I'm *waiting*."

"Goodness, Mister So-and-so," said Hattie. "What big ears you have."

Tennyson smiled and ducked her chin into her chest.

"And what big feet you have!" shouted Hattie. "And what big teeth—"

"This is *not* a joke," thundered Aunt Henrietta. "I expect you to take my instruction seriously, as though your life depended on it. As though the very fate of Aigredoux depended on it! All of our fates depend on you taking my instruction seriously."

The girls glanced at each other.

"Sorry," said Hattie.

"That's better," said Aunt Henrietta. "Now, it is important that you always speak in a soft voice. That way a man will have to lean in closer to hear you. It also attracts attention to your pretty mouths. It's a very alluring habit."

"But what if you have stinky breath?" asked Hattie, a look of genuine concern on her face.

Just then, a knock sounded on the front door.

"Stay here," said Aunt Henrietta as she swept out of the room, sliding the door not quite shut behind her.

"Mornin', ma'am," came a man's voice from the front porch. "We're here to pick up the marble."

"Oh," said Aunt Henrietta, her voice flat. "Yes. Come in."

Two men in work clothes clomped past the ladies' parlor, and the girls shot up off the bench and peeked around the not-quite-shut door to see what would happen. The men climbed up the grand staircase, and with two long, rusty crowbars they pried up marble from ten of the stairs at the top, revealing the wood beneath. They heaved the surprised slabs down the stairs and piled them on the front lawn.

When this was done, one of the men handed Aunt Henrietta a handful of damp bills.

"Five dollars?" she cried. "Is that all? Do you know how much this marble is *worth*? Our ancestors stripped down three châteaus in France to get it!"

"That don't mean a lot these days, does it, ma'am," said one of the men.

"That's *quite* incorrect," called out Uncle Twigs from under his net in his study. "You meant to say, 'That *doesn't* mean a lot these days.'"

When the workers left, it was quiet in the hallway for a

minute and for the first time since they arrived at Aigredoux, Tennyson felt bad for her aunt. She could feel Henrietta's bitterness seeping through the door. Then the door slid open and Aunt Henrietta told them:

"Your lessons are done for the day. Amuse yourselves, but do not go into the rooms that are under construction. Do not bother Uncle Twigs. And do not bother *me*."

And she swept up the splintering, balding grand staircase to her bedroom.

When Aunt Henrietta cried, she looked a lot like Emery, Tennyson thought.

✦✦✦

"Let's play hide-and-seek," said Hattie. "I want to hide first. You be it."

"Okay," said Tennyson. They agreed that Tennyson should count to a hundred, since Aigredoux was so big.

A hundred seconds passed. Tennyson tiptoed up the wooden stairs of the grand staircase. There were hardly any marble ones left, and Tennyson could sense somehow that the house was embarrassed.

Upstairs, every door with its upside-down lock was closed, and the hallway felt like a riddle. Tennyson turned the knob on the first one, to one of the forbidden rooms, and tried to push it open.

Something on the other side pushed back. Tennyson got it to open a crack and she peered inside. A carpet of *vines* had grown against the door. They had crawled up the front of the house and in through some broken panes in the window and devoured nearly everything inside. Leaves and tendrils covered every inch of a bed in the corner, from its claw feet to the tips of the turreted bedposts. The vines rooted two chairs to the floor, and huge, brilliant green ferns had sprang out of the seat cushions. All of the leaves seemed to turn their faces in surprise toward the intruder and Tennyson quickly pulled the door shut, in case those vines got any ideas about swallowing up the hallway too.

She turned the knob on the next door and the room behind this door was black, as though thick velvet curtains had been drawn over the windows. Tennyson choked from all of the moldy dust and covered her nose and mouth with her dress. Trailing her fingers over the wall, she walked along the edges of the room in case the middle of the floor was rotten. A scuffling noise came from the far corner.

Hattie, Tennyson thought.

Another scuffling noise pointed her in the right direction and she felt her way through the dark as quietly as possible, and when she thought that she was close enough, she yelled:

"Boo!"

Suddenly there was a great flapping of wings all around Tennyson's head and something got caught in her hair. The creature screeched and yanked while Tennyson screamed and flailed and finally the creature tore free and flew out into the hallway.

A big black bat.

Just then, another scream filled the air, and it took a few seconds for Tennyson to realize that she wasn't the one screaming anymore. It was Hattie. The screams turned into wails and Tennyson ran into the hallway. The window leading to the balcony was halfway open. Tennyson squeezed through it, and there lay Hattie facedown on the floor, a swarm of enormous wasps spiraling around her limp body.

"Get out of here!" shrieked Tennyson, looking around for something to wave at them, to make them go away. Frantically she tore off her own dress and whipped it through the air. The wasps buzzed angrily and one of them stung Tennyson on the cheek. "Get *away*!" she yelled, and lashed the air with her dress until the last of the wasps flew away.

Tennyson rolled Hattie over. Huge red welts covered her sister's face and neck, her hands and arms. Even her eyes were swollen shut.

The window slid up and Aunt Henrietta stormed out. "I told you *never* to come out here," she shouted, and stopped short when she saw Hattie. "God in heaven," she cried, and called for Zulma.

They laid Hattie out on a sheet in Louvenia's room.

"Pull the stingers out," said Zulma, sweat dripping from her brow. "Get 'em all the way out, 'cause sometimes they break off and get stuck," and she and Tennyson and Aunt Henrietta went over every inch of Hattie's little body, pulling out stingers that were as fine as hairs. Then Zulma covered Hattie in a paste made from cider vinegar and baking soda and wrapped her up in the sheet like a mummy. Hattie didn't talk or she couldn't talk; she just cried as well as she could with her eyes swollen shut like that.

"We were just playing hide-and-seek," Tennyson tried to explain.

"She must've tried to hide behind the window shutters," Zulma said. "Those wasps build nests as big as barrels back there."

"*This* is what happens to little girls who don't listen," said Aunt Henrietta, regaining her icy composure now that the emergency was subsiding. Then she looked at Tennyson and gasped. Tennyson looked down and saw with shame that she was completely naked.

"Savages," cried Aunt Henrietta. "You're both *savages*!" Then something else caught her attention. "What is this? And *this*?" she cried, snatching up the pages of harp music scattered around the edges of the room.

"They're just stories I wrote," said Tennyson, her heart pounding in fear now. There was something unhinged in Aunt Henrietta's anger, like a pot of boiling oil about to overflow.

"You are a *very* bad girl," shouted Aunt Henrietta, tearing around the room and wadding all of Tennyson's stories into a ball. "This music belonged to your ancestor, Louvenia Fontaine. Is this how you treat your family's legacies?"

"I'm sorry!" cried Tennyson. "I didn't know."

"Put on a dress, for heaven's sake," yelled Aunt Henrietta, and she charged out of the room, still clutching the ball of papers.

Hattie snuffled miserably from inside her cocoon.

"That woman's sure got her work cut out for her with the two of you," said Zulma, dabbing a little of the baking soda mixture around Hattie's eyes.

"But it was an accident," said Tennyson shakily. "We were trying to stay out of the way."

"Oh, I ain't talkin' 'bout the bee stings or you ruinin' that music or anything like that," Zulma said. "I know for a fact that she was hopin' you would be the salvation of Aigredoux, and that's gonna take a *whole* lotta work."

"What do you mean?" asked Tennyson.

"Miz Henrietta and Mister Thomas couldn't have children of their own," Zulma said. "So you're her last hope, voodoo girl. I know how that woman's mind works. Right now she's thinkin' that if she makes the two of you into ladies, you'll catch and marry some gentlemen rich enough to save the big house from fallin' down to the ground. And maybe even bring the Fontaine name back from the dead."

Tennyson didn't know what to say. She thought about her aunt's silly lesson that morning, the one about saying lovely things about Apollo to gentlemen suitors, and she could hardly believe that this was Aunt Henrietta's grand scheme to save Aigredoux.

"But we don't even *live* here," she said finally.

"You do now," said Zulma. "And you're Fontaines, and there ain't no other Fontaines left except you-all. To Miz Henrietta, that means it all comes down to you, to keep the family goin' and Aigredoux standin'. That's her life's purpose, and she means business. She can't go on sellin' the marble off the stairs forever. Why, this whole house used to be made of fine white marble! Every floor and windowsill and mantel. They've been sellin' it off for generations to make ends meet, and now it's almost gone."

Tennyson pulled her knees into her chest and wrapped her arms around them. A memory jammed itself into her mind all of a sudden, one about a walk she'd taken with her father in the woods around Innisfree.

It had been a late-autumn afternoon, and dead leaves and soft pine needles crunched beneath their feet. Suddenly Emery stopped in his tracks.

"Don't move," he'd told Tennyson. "I see a bear trap."

And then he hit the trap again and again with a heavy branch until it snapped shut with a deathly rusty clang.

"But what if a bear comes?" Tennyson worried.

"Then he'll come," said Emery. "And go. But what if Jos had come along and gotten caught in that trap? A dog will chew off his own leg to get out of a trap, and we wouldn't want Jos to have to do that, would we?"

"No," Tennyson had said. She didn't want that to happen to Jos, but something else disturbed her. Her father walked on but Tennyson didn't move.

"What is it, baby?" he asked, turning around.

"Why weren't you worried that *I* would get caught in that trap?" she asked. "Or Hattie."

The sun glinted through the trees, and a warm yellow line glowed around the edges of Emery's body.

"Because you're my brave, strong girls," he answered. "You're too smart to get caught in a big trap like that. And I know that you can take care of yourselves."

But now Emery was gone, leaving his brave, strong girls in the jaws of a different sort of trap. And now they were going to find out if their father had been right, if they really could take care of themselves.

Tennyson looked at Zulma. Why did the woman stay at Aigredoux? Why would anyone who had a *choice* stay at Aigredoux?

"Why do you stay here?" she asked Zulma abruptly.

"Huh?"

"You can leave Aigredoux anytime you want, and it's so awful here."

Zulma stared at her.

"Let me tell you this, voodoo girl," she said. "My family's been laborin' here for seven generations. For one hundred and thirty years, we've been pourin' our blood, tears, and sweat into this land. You think we put in all the agony and work just to pack up and go off somewhere and start from scratch?"

"I only meant—"

"There's more of my family's bones buried out back than there are Fontaine bones. Aigredoux belongs just as much to me as it does to you—more so, maybe. And don't you forget it. I ain't goin' anywhere."

And with that Zulma reached over and plucked the stinger out of the welt on Tennyson's cheek.

❖❖❖

That night Zulma left an oil lamp on the floor so Tennyson could keep an eye on Hattie. Tennyson poured spoonfuls of water down her sister's throat. At midnight, Tennyson saw Hattie's eyes gleam through their slitted lids. She was awake.

"I hate it here," Hattie said. "I want Jos."

"I know," said Tennyson. "Soon."

"Aigredoux hates us," said Hattie.

"It does," said Tennyson. "But it doesn't at the same time."

"What do you mean?"

"I can't really explain it," said Tennyson, and when Hattie closed her eyes again, Tennyson thought about what she had said and tried to figure out what she *did* mean.

Aigredoux had flung hateful things in their direction, like wasps and bats and rotten floors that waited in silent glee for little girls to fall through them. It pushed its way into Tennyson's dreams and made her see funerals and spiders.

But there were nicer things too, in the dream and in real life. In the dream there were red lacquer boxes and doves and gold-covered webs. In real life the house pulled the vines back from the windows so the girls could see outside. It was trying to let the light in. Maybe the house was trying to tell them something or give them something.

Suddenly Tennyson sat straight up. She had an idea.

Maybe Aigredoux was trying to give her a way to get Sadie back.

She thought about this for a while. The idea was a far-fetched one, it would probably never work. But the more she mulled it over, the more she saw that it *might* work.

Just try it, she told herself. *You've got nothing to lose.*

This was true. After all, Tennyson had already lost one of the most important things a girl could lose, her mother.

And now she had a choice. She could do nothing and see where the current took her. Or she could take this strange gift from the house and try to help bring Sadie home.

Moonlight streamed in and made a silver puddle on the floor. Tennyson pressed her hand into the light. She almost felt a subtle heartbeat in the floor, the pulse of Aigredoux under her palm.

Then she got Sadie's pen and began to write.

Chapter Eight

ZIPPORAH

It was a week before Tennyson was ready to carry out her idea, the idea that Aigredoux had given her. And she had to keep it a secret too, even from Hattie. Like Sadie had said, Hattie was an open field with no fences, and she couldn't keep a secret. But Tennyson's plan had to be jealously guarded from Aunt Henrietta, who would most certainly tear it to pieces or crumple it into a wad. Aunt Henrietta did not want Sadie to come back, so she and Tennyson were enemies in this fight. Zulma was in Aunt Henrietta's corner and the secret had to be kept from her too.

So every night that week, Tennyson waited until Hattie fell asleep and the house was silent, and then she wrote, because writing was the main part of her plan. But when the writing was done and Tennyson was pleased with the words on the back of the brittle harp music pages, it was time to trust another person with her secret.

Every time I come in here, you're settin' in front of that window and smokin' that pipe. What're you starin' at all day?

I'm starin' at Time passin'.

Zipporah.

Aunt Henrietta was busy with writing of her own, and although she didn't know it, this was also part of Tennyson's plan. Every morning Aunt Henrietta sat in the ladies' parlor and wrote letters on that thin blue paper and she stuffed each of these letters into thin blue envelopes until there was a tall stack of them on her desk, dusted with fine plaster specks like powdered sugar on a cruller.

Finally, the stack was ready.

"Tennyson," called Aunt Henrietta, who had barely talked to her niece all week, since the wasps had happened. "Take these to the post office."

"*Do* wait," called Uncle Twigs from under his net in the gentlemen's parlor. "I have something as well."

"Just this one letter?" Tennyson asked when Uncle Twigs handed her a single letter, sealed with a stamped blot of red wax.

"Yes, child."

"But you've been writing all week," Tennyson said.

"I am *quite* particular about the phrasing of my correspondences," said Uncle Twigs. "I have to set a superior example.

After all, I *am* the president of the Louisiana Society for the Strict Enforcement of the Proper Use of the English Language."

When she was outside, Tennyson pulled a sheaf of papers out of the front of her dress and added them to the stack of letters. It was hot outside, and her body was damp and some of the ink from the papers had bled onto her stomach. She had to be careful with these words and keep them on the paper where they belonged.

Most girls would be scared to walk alone down that stretch of bones and steam and marble tombs, but these things made Tennyson sad, not scared. She was sad for the trees that hadn't wanted to live anymore and bleached themselves into brittle white bones. She was sad for Bon Vivant and wondered what it had done to deserve a fire and why God left the columns there as a reminder, like a branded face. And she was sad for the people in those white marble tombs above the ground and imagined that they must be sleeping very badly under all that hot sun.

But the sadness went away when she smelled the apple tobacco coming through the screen of the post office.

Zipporah Tweed stood up when Tennyson walked in.

"Mornin', Miz Tennyson," he said, lifting the brim of his striped railroad cap.

"I have my aunt Henrietta's letters," Tennyson told him. "And one from Uncle Thomas too."

Zipporah examined Uncle Twigs's letter and chuckled. "Did you see who he's scoldin' this time? President Hoover. He gets a letter every month from Mister Thomas, complainin' 'bout the grammar in poor Mister Hoover's speeches." He shoved the letter along with Aunt Henrietta's blue missives into a burlap sack. "Is that everythin'?"

"No," said Tennyson. "I have something else."

"Well, what is it?"

Tennyson looked at Zipporah solemnly. "I need to know first if you can keep a secret."

" 'Course I can," said Zipporah. "I know every secret worth knowin' in Ascension Parish. And I keep 'em all right here under my hat. That's why it has to be so big—and I *never* take it off."

Tennyson showed him the papers, her secret writing.

"These need to get sent to New York City," she told him.

"I swear," he said, setting his pipe down. "What's all this?"

"It's a story," Tennyson said. "Actually, it's the first chapter of a book, but it stands alone as a story too."

"Who wrote it?" asked Zipporah, flipping over one of the pages and looking at the harp music printed on the other side.

"I did. It's about my family in the old days."

"And why does it have to get sent all the way to New York City?"

Tennyson took a deep breath. "I'm sending it to the *Sophisticate* magazine," she said. "I want them to print it."

"Whew, that's awfully ambitious of you," Zipporah said, smiling. "But why's this all gotta be a secret?"

"Because my aunt Henrietta can't find out," Tennyson explained. "She'll put a stop to my plan. It's *very* important that this story gets published in that magazine. If it does, my mother will read it and it might make her come home."

Zipporah rubbed his beard. "I don't get it," he said.

"It's hard to explain," said Tennyson. "But I know that wherever she is, my mother will read the magazine. She reads it all the time. It's her whole life. And if my story gets published there, there's something in it that will make her want to come back."

"What, like a code or somethin'?" asked Zipporah.

"Sort of."

"Why won't you tell me?"

"It's private," said Tennyson.

"All right, fair enough," said Zipporah. "But why would your aunt try to put a stop to your plan?"

"Because my aunt doesn't want my mother to come back," Tennyson said. "She hates my mother and wants me and my sister to stay at Aigredoux. Even though she hates us too, I think."

Zipporah looked down at the ragged, peculiar story on the counter. "I swear," he said. "Miz Tennyson, I'm sure that you got a real good idea. But I hate to see you get your hopes all up and then get 'em dashed. What makes you think that the magazine would print your story in the first place?"

"Because it's good," said Tennyson.

Zipporah stared at her.

"You sure are an old child," he said finally.

"Read the story for yourself if you want," Tennyson said impatiently.

So Zipporah sat back down in his rocking chair behind the counter with Tennyson's pages and soon the sweet-smelling white smoke curled up from his pipe. There was no sound except the turning of those pages and the cane blowing in the field. Tennyson sat on the floor and rested her chin on the windowsill and looked outside while Zipporah read. When she stopped hearing the pages turning, Tennyson looked back at Zipporah.

He took a deep puff on his pipe and let the smoke filter out of his mouth very slowly and he looked at Tennyson for a long time. Then he got up from his rocking chair, put the story into an envelope, and wrote on the front of it:

> Editor
> *Sophisticate* Magazine
> New York City, NY USA

On the back, he wrote:

> c/o Zipporah Tweed, Postmaster
> Ascension Parish Post Office
> Louisiana, USA

It went into the burlap sack, on top of Aunt Henrietta's blue letters.

"Godspeed, story," Zipporah said, settling back down into his chair. "You know, you won't never find comfort like the comfort of your mother again, not if you live to be a hundred. I'll pray that it works out for you, Miz Tennyson."

They watched the shadows of the clouds move across the cane fields.

"Zipporah," said Tennyson.

"Mmm-hmm."

"Doesn't it make you sad to look out over the fields and see the graveyard over there? And Bon Vivant, and the bone forest?"

"Nope," Zipporah answered.

"Why not?" Tennyson said. "All those things make me sad."

"That's all part of life, honey," answered Zipporah. "Everything has its time, and then it has to move on and make way for new things to have their time." He reached back and picked up his copy of *The Poetic Works of Alfred, Lord Tennyson*.

"Listen to this," he said, and he recited,

> "Nothing will die;
> All things will change
> Thro' eternity.
> 'Tis the world's winter;
> Autumn and summer
> Are gone long ago;
> Earth is dry to the centre,
> But spring, a new comer,
> A spring rich and strange,
> Shall make the winds blow
> Round and round,
> Thro' and thro',
>   Here and there,
>   Till the air
> And the ground
> Shall be fill'd with life anew."

He closed the book.

"Did your mother ever read you that poem?" he asked.

Tennyson nodded.

"Do you believe what Mister Alfred, Lord Tennyson is sayin' in it?"

"I don't know," said Tennyson. "In most places you see spring come after winter and everything is fresh and new. But not here. We don't really have seasons, and things don't seem to die all the way *or* begin anew. Things linger on. Everything seems trapped in time."

Zipporah nodded. "Time *does* sort of follow its own rules down here, doesn't it," he said. "But that's what makes it so interesting to watch."

They sat together in silence for the rest of the afternoon and looked at the emerald green cane blowing in the hot breeze.

Part Two

Chapter Nine

BARTHOLOMEW

Many worlds away, in roaring New York City, a fat man named Bartholomew Prentiss sat at a table in a fancy restaurant.

Every day he sat in this fancy restaurant, called Sardi's, all by himself—which is just how he liked it. And every day, as he sat there, he would eat three glazed pork chops with a little pearl onion on top of each, like a crown. And while he was eating those pork chops, he'd drink three martinis with three olives in each. Inside each of those olives was a piece of blue cheese. Bartholomew Prentiss was a man who liked everything just so. And everyone at Sardi's knew not to disturb him when he was sitting there all by himself.

Well, *almost* everyone.

"MISTER Prentiss," boomed a young man from across the restaurant, causing Bartholomew to jump up in his seat and spill his martini all over the place.

The young man sailed over and sat down at Bartholomew's table. The waiters stopped in their tracks and gawked. No one had ever before dared disturb the pork-chop-eating activities of Bartholomew Prentiss, editor in chief of the *Sophisticate* magazine!

"Who are you and why are you sitting at my table?" Bartholomew snapped, patting his rather robust stomach with a napkin.

"Allow me to introduce myself," the young man said, tightening his neat red-polka-dotted bow tie. "I am none other than W. Baxter Alexander." He sat back looking very pleased with himself.

"Who?" barked Bartholomew.

"W. Baxter Alexander," repeated the young man, clearly annoyed. "The writer. The *famous* writer."

"Never heard of you," sniffed Bartholomew looking miserably at his martini-drenched pork chop. "Now, could you kindly decamp from my table?"

"Oh, I'm sure that you must have!" cried the man. "I am the most important writer of my generation. At least, that's what all of my reviews say. And I have a *brilliant* idea for a story for your magazine."

A buzzing fly came and sat right on top of the pork chop.

"Okay, picture this," continued W. Baxter Alexander breezily. "It's set today, in 1932. America's in the middle of a depression.

Everyone's poor and miserable. Now, the way *I* see it, what we need to do is put the *fun* back into being poor and miserable! We need a character who'll tell people, 'Hey! We're all eating dirt! Let's find a way to enjoy it!' We'll give 'em *Willie, America's Favorite Hobo.* And every month we'll have a new story about Willie having adventures across the country. You know, shaking things up in shantytowns, rowdying around on the railroads—that sort of thing."

Bartholomew's face grew bright red and he stood up. The waiters poked each other because they knew that the show was *really* about to begin.

"How dare you!" he cried. "Don't you know who I *am*? I am Bartholomew Prentiss, editor of the *Sophisticate,* not the proprietor of some cheap comics page! And *this* is what I think of your idea, you impudent pup!" And with that, he picked up his end of the tablecloth and the pork chop sloshed across the table and neatly into W. Baxter Alexander's lap.

Everyone in the restaurant gasped, but Bartholomew paid them no attention as he snatched his special red-velvet-lined cape from a hook on the wall and swept out. No one dared point out to him that it was a rather hot afternoon, being Indian summer and all. But Bartholomew put on his special cape anyway and stomped out into the dirty, bustling New York City street.

My poor little pork chop, he thought as he strode along. *Wasted on the lap of that horrid little fraud, Baxter Waxter, or whatever his name was.* And to make things worse, he was still hungry. He saw a little pork chop glaze clinging to his cape. Once he'd licked it all off, he made his way to a hot dog stand on the corner.

A weaselly little man stood behind the cart, wearing a paper hat and clutching a pair of tongs. The cart bore a sign that announced:

Joe's Dogs

"Good afternoon, Joseph," said Bartholomew. "I've been deprived of my lunch and shall require sustenance from your establishment."

"Name's Joe," said the man. "I'm gettin' tired of tellin' you that every day. And I don't understand a darn word you just said."

"Just give me four hot dogs," said Bartholomew snippily. He flung his cape behind his shoulders and chewed away, thinking melancholy thoughts.

"Quit leanin' on my cart," said Joe. "You're rollin' it down the street."

"A thousand apologies," said Bartholomew. "I was just pondering the state of American literature today. I've said it before, my dear Joseph, but this time I really mean it: American literature is dead."

"Huh?" said Joe, fishing around in a watery vat and producing a fifth hot dog for Bartholomew.

"There aren't any good writers out there today," explained Bartholomew. While he was deeply intolerant of W. Baxter Alexander types, Bartholomew liked to believe that he was a friend to the common man, the man on the street. And because of this, Joe the hot dog man got treated to Bartholomew's musings nearly every day.

"I can't remember the last time someone sent me something I liked," Bartholomew went on. "All I get is tripe, tripe, tripe. The whole point of the *Sophisticate* is to discover, nurture, and publish genius! Art, Joseph! And instead I'm inflicted with mediocre snivelers and braggarts. It is a true crisis, in every sense of the word."

"If that's the worst of your problems, you won't catch me cryin' a river for you," crabbed Joe.

"Well, if I don't find a decent writer soon, I'm toast," Bartholomew said darkly, wiping his mouth on the corner of his cape and letting his belt out another notch. "Done for, finished."

"Welcome to the club," said Joe. "You owe me extra for the ketchup."

Bartholomew paid him extra for the ketchup and swept up the street, his red-velvet-lined cape billowing out behind him.

And then he marched straight back to his office to steer the fate of American literature away from the rocks of disaster.

❖❖❖

The office of Bartholomew Prentiss might well have been considered the eighth wonder of the world. It supposedly had walls and floors like other offices, although no one had seen evidence of them in years. This was because tall stacks of manuscripts and books towered to the ceiling along every wall and covered nearly every inch of floor. In order to get from one side of the room (the door) to the other (Bartholomew's desk), you had to squeeze through a meandering path that had been carved through that forest of paper.

"Joy," bellowed Bartholomew, shaking his cape around expectantly.

Joy—or Miss Joy Goodenough if you want to be formal about it—was Bartholomew's secretary, and it was her job to take his special cape from him and hand him the latest manuscripts that had been mailed in.

"Joy!" he shouted again, and when he got no response, he crammed himself through the maze, going sideways like a crab.

He heard a scuffling noise at the end of the path and steeled himself to encounter a rat or some such but instead found Miss Goodenough sitting at his big desk, engrossed in a manuscript.

"And just *what* do you think you're doing?" bellowed Bartholomew.

"*Oh!*" yelped Miss Goodenough and shot out of Bartholomew's chair, which was, of course, lined with red velvet. The manuscript fell to the floor in a flurry of pages. Miss Goodenough was always dropping things in this manner. In fact, everything about her was lopsided and topsy-turvy. Her glasses always sat askew on her face and her hairdo leaned to one side like the Tower of Pisa. Even one of her legs was shorter than the other, causing her to totter from one side to the other as she walked.

"I beg your pardon, sir," she said meekly, lurching around the desk to collect his red-velvet-lined cape.

"How *dare* you sit at my desk," said Bartholomew. "And you *never* read my submissions! Why, I didn't even know that you were literate!" he added nastily.

Miss Goodenough blushed. "Well, sir, it was just such an intriguing-looking manuscript that I couldn't help—"

"Bring me a coffee and a Danish," Bartholomew interrupted, settling fatly into his chair. "I didn't get a lot of lunch today."

"Yes, sir," said Miss Goodenough. And she disappeared into the paper maze, her orthopedic shoes squeaking like little mice.

Bartholomew sighed. Miss Goodenough had left a stack of newly arrived manuscripts on his desk. He picked up the top one, read the first page, snickered, and threw it into his special trash can, onto which he'd taped pictures of his most hated authors. The next manuscript was so terrible that Bartholomew lumbered over to the only exposed window in his office and threw it out. The pages fluttered like confetti through the air and onto the street below. He sat down again.

Suddenly Miss Goodenough ran back through the labyrinth, her shoes blatting away.

"Sir!" she cried. "Mr. Nusselbaum is coming this way!"

Mr. Nusselbaum was the terrifying owner of the magazine. His face was always red as a tomato, and he carried a big tin of blood pressure pills with him wherever he went.

"Ohhh," said Bartholomew, and he lurched out of his chair and wedged himself under his desk. It was rather snug but still a most effective hideaway, for no one ever suspected that Bartholomew Prentiss could actually *fit* under there.

"Tell him I'm still at lunch," he gasped to Miss Goodenough. "And pass me that Danish."

"Good afternoon, Mr. Nusselbaum," trilled Miss Goodenough from somewhere inside the manuscript labyrinth.

"I'm going to get a bulldozer to come clean out this dump," growled Mr. Nusselbaum, rattling his pill tin around. "Where's Big Boy?"

"I'm afraid that Mr. Prentiss is still out to lunch," said Miss Goodenough pleasantly. "Can I pass on a message from you, sir?"

"Yeah," said Mr. Nusselbaum. "You sure can, toots. Tell him that he'd better breathe life back into the next issue of the *Sophisticate* or I'm gonna can him. I want him to find a big story, something larger than life—and it has to be an all-American tale. I want history! Romance! Tragedy! All rolled up into one story. And if he can't rummage up a story like that, tell Big Boy that I'll find someone who can."

"Yes, sir," said Miss Goodenough, scribbling on her pad. "History, romance, tragedy—or no job. I'll relay the message."

"Philistine," muttered Bartholomew to himself, one of his knees shoved up against his nose. "Desecrator of art!"

"He's gone, sir," said Miss Goodenough, peeking under the desk.

"Good, help me out," coughed Bartholomew, but it was soon

unhappily discovered that he was *quite* stuck, as Uncle Twigs would have put it. "Pull my leg," he told Miss Goodenough, but when she did as she was told, the desk came along with Bartholomew and both were dragged several feet across the floor.

"Oh dear, oh dear," said Miss Goodenough as she drummed her fingers on her thin parched lips. "I'll just run out and get a handyman who can lift the desk up off of you."

This is the most dreadful day in recent history, thought Bartholomew, and he felt very sorry for himself. Of course, he wasn't too cramped to eat the Danish, but once that was gone he had to find another way to console and amuse himself.

Then something caught his attention.

He reached out and snatched up a sheet of paper from the floor. Strangely, harp music covered one side of it. On the other was a handwritten page of a story.

"How wonderfully creepy," Bartholomew said to himself. The paper had fallen out from the manuscript that Miss Goodenough had been reading. Written-on harp music littered the whole floor around the desk. He grasped around until he found the first page, which proclaimed:

"The Tragedy of Louvenia Fontaine"
By Tennyson Fontaine
CHAPTER ONE

"And what deliciously awful child scrawl," said Bartholomew. "I bet old Mr. Fontaine is crazy as a loon." But since he had nothing else to do down there under his desk, he began to read.

Ten minutes later, Miss Goodenough returned with a handyman and the two of them were treated to the most astonishing
sight. Bartholomew's desk was literally jumping up and down on
the ground. *Wump, wump, wump.*

"Calm down, sir—we're here!" called Miss Goodenough.

"It's about time," cried Bartholomew from under the desk.
"I need to dictate a letter to you right away."

"Yes, sir," said Miss Goodenough, wielding her pencil and
pad of paper. The handyman put his foot on Bartholomew and
tugged the desk upward.

"Oww—that's my *clavicle*!" howled Bartholomew at the
handyman. "Watch it, you blunderer! Joy, pay attention! Here's
the letter."

> Dear Mr. Fontaine:
>
> Congratulations. The *Sophisticate* would
> like to honor you by publishing the
> first chapter of your book, titled *The
> Tragedy of Louvenia Fontaine*. It will
> appear in the next issue and enclosed
> is a check for ten dollars. Please send
> the next installment immediately. If
> we like what you send us, we will
> publish the whole book, chapter by
> chapter.
>
> Very truly yours,
> *Bartholomew Prentiss*
> Editor in Chief

The handyman finally wrenched the desk off Bartholomew Prentiss, editor in chief, nurturer of genius. He spilled out into a puddle on the floor and breathed the free air.

"Now, then—where does Mr. Fontaine live?" he asked.

Miss Goodenough searched around on the floor for the manuscript's envelope.

"It only says: *care of Zipporah Tweed, Postmaster, Ascension Parish Post Office, Louisiana, USA,*" she reported.

"Well, isn't that just *dandy,*" said Bartholomew. "An authentic backwaters writer! How rare these days. His writing is wonderfully plain—you know I hate it when writers are fancy for the sake of being fancy. *And* Mr. Fontaine doesn't use too many adverbs—you know how I *detest* adverbs," he added, his eyes narrowing.

"I *told* you it was good," said Miss Goodenough.

"My dear Miss Goodenough." Bartholomew beamed, sitting up and clutching the harp-music manuscript in his plump little fingers. "You and this young Fontaine chap from Louisiana may have just saved us our hides."

Chapter Ten

SISYPHUS

Several weeks went by, and some things happened at faraway Aigredoux and others did not. What did not happen: Emery did not find Sadie. At least, if he did find Sadie, they did not come and take Tennyson and Hattie back to Innisfree.

What did happen: it started to rain and once it started, it did not stop. The rain fell for a day and then two days and then a week and Aigredoux began to creak and lean and groan. It soaked up the rain like a sponge and its walls and ceilings swelled and glistened with wet.

Zulma and Aunt Henrietta stood out on the front porch behind the columns and watched the levee warily.

"It will hold, won't it, Zulma," worried Aunt Henrietta.

"I sure hope so," said Zulma.

Aunt Henrietta wrapped her arms around herself. "Do you remember what happened to Magnolia Hall?"

"Mmm-hmm," said Zulma.

"What happened to Magnolia Hall?" asked Hattie, coming out and standing behind Zulma. These days, Hattie was never far away from Zulma. Her wasp stings had healed, but after her trauma she needed comfort, a mother. And while Sadie was gone, Hattie chose Zulma. Even though Zulma was all gristle and angles and bones, Hattie drank up any drops of softness she could wring out of the woman. Even if most of it came from the warm colors of Zulma's apron and dress and not Zulma herself.

"Lord, you're just like a haint, sneakin' up on people like that," cried Zulma. Aunt Henrietta didn't even acknowledge Hattie's presence.

"Sorry," Hattie said. "But what happened to Magnolia Hall?"

"The river came right out of its bed and swallowed it up durin' a big storm," said Zulma. "But that was a long time ago, before the levee got built."

Aunt Henrietta shuddered. "Let's go inside," she said. "We all have work to do."

In fact, the rain gave everyone at Aigredoux a great deal of work in addition to worrying that the Mississippi would get hungry for the house.

It was Hattie and Tennyson's job to place an armada of

chipped mason jars and pots and pans under holes in Aigre-doux's soft leaking roof and ceilings, and there were many of these holes. The jars filled up quickly, and the girls had to run from room to room to pick them up and empty them out onto the front lawn. And when they finished with the last room, they had to start all over again with the first.

"You have *quite* a Sisyphian task, I'm afraid," observed Uncle Twigs, whose job it was to hide all of his important papers under the desk and chairs in his study and make sure they didn't get dripped on.

"What does that mean?" asked Hattie, lugging a pan of water down the Hall of Ancestors to the front porch. Zulma had covered the portraits in wax paper, but even so the faces in the paintings still looked miserable.

"Sisyphus was *quite* an evil king in ancient Greece," explained Uncle Twigs, wringing out his mosquito net. "When Sisyphus died and went to the underworld, he was forced to roll *quite* a large rock up a steep hill. But whenever he reached the top of the hill, the rock always escaped him and rolled back down to the bottom. So he would have to begin all over again, and this went on forever."

A chunk of damp plaster fell from the ceiling and splatted onto the floor.

In the ladies' parlor, Aunt Henrietta tried to write her usual pile of letters to Washington, but the water in the air curled the paper and bled the ink. So she had to wrap her writing materials up in wax paper and put them away.

Unfortunately, this meant that her primary occupation became disapproving of her nieces. She stood in the doorway of the parlor and watched the girls scurry out onto the porch with their rain-filled pots and pans.

"Hold it right there," she said to Tennyson. "What happened to the back of your dress?"

Tennyson stopped. "It ripped the first night we got here," she said.

"That was an expensive dress," snapped Aunt Henrietta. "You are a very destructive girl. I'm clearly falling behind in my reforming education. When you and your sister replace those pans, come back here to the parlor. I'm resuming your lessons immediately."

Ten minutes later, the girls were seated on the bench in the ladies' parlor.

"Today we're going to learn about the etiquette of courtship," Aunt Henrietta explained.

"Courtship—is that like a tennis court on a boat?" asked Hattie.

"No," said Aunt Henrietta crossly. "*Courtship* means when a gentleman caller comes to pay a visit to woo you. We're going to go over the rules." She drew aside the curtain in front of the window and looked out toward the river. Bondurant sat in a puddle on the front porch outside the window and stared up at them resentfully.

"But we don't know any gentlemen callers," Hattie pointed out.

"Not yet," said Aunt Henrietta. "But there are still viable candidates in Ascension Parish, some young men worthy of a Fontaine match."

Then she stared silently at the levee for a few minutes.

"Is the water coming over?" asked Hattie.

Aunt Henrietta snapped back to life.

"We'll start with the courtship candle," she said. "When a gentleman caller comes, either I or your uncle Thomas will place a candle in this holder here."

"You meant to say 'your uncle Thomas or I,' " called Uncle Twigs from across the hallway.

Aunt Henrietta sighed.

Then she showed the girls a candlestick on the sideboard. "If we approve of the gentleman caller, we will place a tall candle there and he can stay until it has burned all the way down. If we do not approve of him, you will see us place a short candle there. He'd have to leave quite quickly in that case."

Hattie sat back, her arms folded across her chest. "I sure hope that there're only short candles in the house," she muttered.

Aunt Henrietta paced back and forth in front of the window, staring at the levee.

"I just *know* the water's going to come over," she fretted. "*Everything* is against us," she added ominously and then, without another word, she walked out of the ladies' parlor and right out the front door of the house.

Hattie and Tennyson ran over to the window and watched

their aunt stalk through the steam and sheets of rain down through the gnarled lazy-oak tunnel to investigate the levee.

"I guess the lesson's over," Hattie said. "Let's go find Zulma."

Zulma sat in the silver pantry, polishing a huge urn with a cloth. The girls sat on the floor amidst a jumble of mismatched silver dishes.

"Why are there dents in all the silver?" asked Hattie.

" 'Cause it was buried for a long time," answered Zulma, rubbing away.

"Buried in the ground?" asked Hattie. "Like pirate treasure?"

"Mmm-hmm," Zulma said. "Durin' the Civil War. When the Yankee troops started comin' up the river and takin' over the big houses, the soldiers looted all the rich stuff. So your Miz Julia made their slaves bury all the silver out in the backyard where the soldiers wouldn't find it. Then, when the war was over, Mister Atlas and Miz Julia had to dig up the silver themselves, and a lot of it got bent outta shape. They never did find all of it either."

"Wait!" Hattie yelled. "You mean there's still *treasure* out in the backyard?"

"That's exactly what I mean."

Hattie ran out of the room and Zulma and Tennyson heard the back door slap shut. Then there was nothing but the sound of the *drip drip drip* from the ceiling and the quiet squeak of Zulma's rag on the dented silver.

"So, voodoo girl," said Zulma. "Any more dreams 'bout the big house in the old days?"

"No," said Tennyson.

They were quiet as Zulma worked until Tennyson said, "Is that true, what you told Hattie just now? Is there really still silver out in the yard?"

"Naw," said Zulma, putting the urn up onto the shelf and reaching for a tray. "The slaves who buried it, they'd go dig it up at night, specially toward the end of the war, when Miz Julia couldn't control them anymore. That silver paid for a whole lotta escape trips up north. What's here in this room is all that's left."

"So why did you lie to Hattie?"

"That girl needs to get outta my hair and get some fresh air, even if it is pourin' outside."

They were quiet again for a minute.

"Zulma," Tennyson said.

"You're gettin' just as pesty as your sister," said Zulma. "What is it?"

"Is the river going to come over the levee and swallow up Aigredoux?"

Zulma didn't even look at her. "Probably," she said.

Tennyson's heart skipped a beat. "Really?"

"Sure," said Zulma. "If not today, then someday. That river's like God. It gives and it takes away. It's been hungry for Aigredoux for a long, long time. God's been callin' for the end of Aigredoux and its kind for almost a hundred years. We fight back, but we're gonna lose in the end."

"But if we're going to lose, then why stay and fight?"

"Because it's home," said Zulma. "There ain't anyplace else for people like us. We're tied up here in the history and the vines and even the air, and there's no gettin' away."

She put the tray back on a high shelf and turned around to face Tennyson.

"Why're you still sittin' there?" she asked. "Do you want me to get you a cushion and some bonbons? Go on and empty those rain jars out."

For the first time in their acquaintance, Tennyson thought that Zulma looked weary and old.

✦✦✦

Eventually the rain wore itself out. It thinned to a drizzle and then to nothing at all. So Tennyson and Hattie got different jobs. Hattie's job was to walk around the yard and stamp out the puddles before mosquitoes could come and lay eggs there. Tennyson's job was to take the mail to Zipporah again. Aunt Henrietta whipped up a fresh batch of indignation and poured it onto her tissue-thin blue paper, and soon a stack of letters was ready to be mailed to Washington, D.C.

The river road was more river than road, and Tennyson's feet turned pruney from wading through all of the puddles. The bone forest had turned into a swamp. The white marble boxes and houses in the graveyard appeared to float in a lake. But after that came the warm, cheerful smell of apple tobacco, and Tennyson ran up the stairs of the post office.

"Mister Tweed," she called. "It's me, Tennyson Fontaine. Did anything come?"

"I swear," said Zipporah from his chair behind the counter. "I thought Ascension Parish was gonna get washed clean away this time."

Tennyson dumped Aunt Henrietta's blue letters onto the counter.

"Please tell me," she said.

"Hmmm," Zipporah said, standing up. "I seem to remember a letter comin' in all the way from New York City for *someone* at Aigredoux. But I could be wrong."

"Really? Did something really come?"

"Just let me look around a moment," Zipporah said. He lifted up a pen on the counter. "Is it under here? Nope. How 'bout here?" he said, lifting up a letter opener.

"Don't tease!" cried Tennyson. "Where is it?"

"Oh, *now* I remember where I put it!" said Zipporah, and he lifted up his blue and white railroad cap, revealing a letter underneath.

Tennyson's voice caught in her dry throat as he handed her the letter and she suddenly needed to seal herself off from the world as she read it. Because she knew that the words written on the letter would tell her whether her mother would come home or not. She ran into the corner and faced the walls.

Zipporah watched her open the note and read it, her hands trembling like water in a glass when a train goes by.

"Well, don't keep me waitin'," he said. "What's it say?"

Tennyson didn't speak for a minute, and when she turned around, there was joy in her face, real joy.

"They're printing my story."

"Kingdom come!" whooped Zipporah, throwing his cap up in the air and coming around the counter.

Tennyson held out the letter for Zipporah to read.

"I've got a confession to make," he said, taking it. "I read it already. I just got so excited when it came that I had to. You ain't mad with me, are you?"

"No," said Tennyson. "I just can't believe that my plan is working."

"You need proof?" asked Zipporah. "Sit tight. Something else came in the envelope with the letter." He reached behind the counter. "Look at this."

He handed her a copy of the *Sophisticate*, dated from a few weeks earlier. Inside, Zipporah had folded down a page that read:

"The Tragedy of Louvenia Fontaine"
By Tennyson Fontaine

> *This is the first installment of a serial.*
> *The next installment will appear in a*
> *future issue.*

Tennyson held the magazine but her fingers could hardly feel the pages. She was still getting used to the fact that she was having everyone else's dreams. First she'd had Aigredoux's dream. And now she was having her mother's dream, Sadie's hungry dream of getting her stories published in the magazine.

"And there's one more surprise," said Zipporah, handing Tennyson a small piece of paper, a long green rectangle.

"What is it?"

"A check!"

Tennyson blinked. "A what?"

"It's money," Zipporah told her. "They're payin' you ten whole dollars for your story."

"But it doesn't look like money."

"Well, you bring it to a bank, and they give you ten dollar bills for it," Zipporah explained.

"You bring it to a what?" asked Tennyson.

Zipporah just looked at her.

"I'll tell you what," he said after a minute, taking the check and putting it in the envelope with the magazine. "Just give that check to your daddy when he comes back to get you. He'll know what to do with it."

He rummaged around on the shelf behind the counter. "In the meantime, this all calls for a celebration," he said, handing her a thick glass bottle. "Have a sip of this."

"What is it?"

"It's Coca-Cola for you," he said. "And Coca-Cola with a little something mixed in for me," he added, producing another bottle.

Tennyson took the bottle from him, and the drink tasted sweet and sticky and tingled her teeth. Zipporah took a long, thirsty swig from his cup and then did a little dance to help Tennyson celebrate. While he danced, he sang:

Old Aunt Maria, jump in the fire.
Fire too hot, jump in the pot.
Pot too black, jump in the crack.
Crack too high, jump in the sky.
Sky too blue, jump in canoe.
Canoe too shallow, jump in the tallow.
Tallow too soft, jump in the loft.
Loft too rotten, jump in the cotton.
Cotton so white, she stay there all night.

Tennyson clapped along and her head started to swim. It felt strange and wonderful to be happy and to have someone feel affection for her again. She wished she knew the words so she could sing along.

Zipporah finished his song and collapsed back into his wicker chair. He picked up his pipe again.

"I swear, I'm too old to kick my heels up like that anymore," he said. "You know, I didn't think it was gonna happen for you. That story was damn good, but there're lots of good stories out there. You've got someone lookin' out for you, from above maybe."

He leaned back and lit his pipe again with a match.

"But my Lord—have you got your work cut out for you now," he said. "This Bartholomew Prentiss wants the next story right away. He clearly don't think you're a child, or he would've thrown your story into the trash, along with your mama's stories and everyone else's. Now I just hope that your mama's readin' that story somewhere and that she gets what you're tryin' to say to her."

"She'll read it," said Tennyson.

The sun was going down and its light burned gold and silver on the leftover rain haze hanging above the cane. Tennyson put the letter into the envelope with the magazine and the check. Tucking the envelope into her dress, she said goodbye and started her walk back up the river road.

As she walked, she heard Zipporah singing a low, very sad song:

> *I said, motherless children sees a hard time*
> *   when mother is gone.*
> *Lord, Lord.*
> *Motherless children sees a hard time when*
> *   mother is gone.*
> *Here they go run from door to door,*
> *But they have nowhere to go.*
> *Nobody treat you like your mother when*
> *   mother is gone.*

The words stayed in her ears all the way home and they were still there when she went to sleep that night.

Chapter Eleven

BEFORE THE STORM

"Tennyson," called Aunt Henrietta from downstairs.

Tennyson rolled over in her bed and opened her eyes. It was still dark out.

"Tennyson Fontaine," came her aunt's voice again. "Come here right now."

She slipped out of the bed and went downstairs to see what Aunt Henrietta wanted. She found the woman sitting in the ladies' parlor, all alone in the dark.

"It's about time," Aunt Henrietta snapped. "How many times do I have to call you?"

"What's happening?" asked Tennyson.

"Zulma needs you in the backyard."

"What for?"

"Why must you girls *always* answer back?" cried Aunt Henrietta. "Just *go*."

So Tennyson stumbled through the dark hallways and out into the backyard.

Suddenly it was broad daylight. Tennyson blinked and shaded her eyes and realized that she had abruptly woken up into a dream. Just when she needed another dream, Aigredoux had slipped like mist into her mind and made her a dream ghost again.

Several peacocks bustled past her. They looked around frantically, as though they didn't know where to go next. Something was wrong.

The back door opened and house servants streamed out of the big house, carrying silver dishes. They ran with these things to the yard and began to dig holes in the ground.

"Stop," shouted a voice from the house, and Atlas Fontaine came running out into the yard. "Not here. The grass will look dug up when the Yankee soldiers get here, and they'll know that things are buried here."

Soldiers! Tennyson thought. So she would be there to see war make its way to Aigredoux. Her heart pounded and she half hoped that the dream would let her wake up before those soldiers arrived.

"Where you want us to put these things then, sir?" one of the slaves asked Atlas, her tray loaded with gleaming silver julep cups.

"In the pig yard, since it's all mud already anyway," he said. "That way the Yankee soldiers won't know anything is there, and besides, they won't want to root around in a pigpen to look."

The slaves looked at each other in despair. They didn't want to root around in the pig yard either. But because they had no choice in this or any other matter, they ran back and forth from the big house into the pig yard, carrying boxes of silverware and teapots and candelabras and even the huge urn that Zulma had been polishing. And they began to dig muddy holes in the rocky, filthy slop.

Julia Fontaine stood like a statue on the back terrace, her arms folded. A servant came out the back door trailing long strands of pearls from her arms. Julia grabbed the pearls.

"Effie, are you crazy, burying pearls in mud?" she snapped. "They'll be ruined forever, you stupid girl. Follow me."

The servant followed Julia inside and so did Tennyson.

Chaos reigned inside the big house. Open trunks stood along all of the walls and the house slaves frantically packed clothes and provisions into these trunks. Someone was taking a journey. The Hall of Ancestors had been stripped bare and the portraits had been stacked five deep against the walls, ready to be stashed in the attic. Even Louvenia's unfinished wedding portrait stood there, covered in a sheer black cloth.

"Everyone out," Julia called. "Except you, Effie."

Tennyson looked at the slave who stayed behind, the one who had almost buried the pearls. Effie wore a black dress with a white apron over it. Her spare, hard face reminded Tennyson of Zulma's. Julia drew all of the curtains across the windows.

"You are never to utter a word about what I'm going to show you," Julia told Effie. She towered at least a foot over her slave. "You are the only one besides Master Atlas and myself who will know about this secret. If it's ever discovered, I will know that *you* are responsible."

"Yes, ma'am," said Effie, looking at the floor.

Julia walked to the paneled wood side of the grand marble staircase. She ran her hands over the panels slowly. Tennyson stood behind her ancestor and watched the woman's hands.

"Here it is," Julia said as her finger detected a tiny hole in one of the panels. Then she ran her finger along a gap between the floorboards and extracted a long, thin knitting needle that had been hidden there. She stuck the needle into the hole and suddenly a door hidden in those panels sprang open, leading underneath the grand marble staircase.

"Now go fetch my jewels," Julia told Effie. The slave ran upstairs and staggered back down with an enormous ivory box. She set it down at Julia's feet.

Julia opened the top and twenty silk-lined shelves automatically slid out in front. Glistening diamonds and rubies the size of cherries filled many of these shelves. Fine pearls coiled like sleeping snakes on top of one another. In the other drawers and compartments: tiaras, bracelets, necklaces, rings, brooches, all crested with sapphires, emeralds, citrine, alexandrite. Julia put the rescued pearl necklace into the box, and then she closed and locked it.

"Follow me," she said as she lit an oil lamp and disappeared through the secret door.

On the other side of the door, a pitch-black spiral stairwell delved deep into the earth below Aigredoux. It might have been the way to Hades, it went that deep. Down they all went, Julia in front with the lamp, followed by Effie, who carried the heavy ivory jewel box. Neither of them knew that an eleven-year-old girl had been dreamed into their world and was following them.

At the bottom of the stairs stood a door with an enormous old lock, like the entrance of a dungeon. Julia reached into her collar and pulled out a string holding a bronze key, and with it she unlocked the great rusty lock. The door creaked open on its hinges, and Effie gasped and dropped the ivory box on the ground.

Inside was a vast treasury of pure gold, thousands and thousands of bars of it, towering far above Tennyson's head. There was so much gold in that room that you couldn't even walk inside. It was absolutely crammed in. The light from Julia's lamp bounced off this gold and Tennyson had to turn away, the blaze of gold was so bright. Like the sun blazing on the gold-covered webs, it was that kind of beauty.

So, this was the money that Emery hated so much. Money made from blood and bones and the emerald green cane that swayed in the fields far above their head, the real world.

"Help me wedge the jewel trunk in there," Julia said. "We should be able to make it fit." The women heaved the ivory chest up and shoved it into the vault. Julia pounded her big square shoulder against it until they could close the door again.

When the mistress and her slave locked the room up and went upstairs and closed the secret panel door in the stairs and opened up all of the curtains again, Aigredoux had already changed.

War was coming.

The house was losing its color, like a woman whose face goes white with fear.

+++

It was suddenly afternoon in the dream, and Tennyson found herself inside the ladies' parlor. Julia sat at a table in the corner playing solitaire, her back erect as a cadet's. Louvenia sat in another corner, sullenly plucking at a harp, the one that still stood in the parlor nearly a hundred years later. She wore a black mourning dress.

"When is Father leaving?" Louvenia asked.

"Later this afternoon," replied Julia.

"How many slaves is he taking?" Louvenia asked, inducing a rather sour chord from the harp.

"All of them, except the house staff," Julia said.

"He's only leaving us ten servants? That's so selfish."

"He has to," Julia said. "Those gunboats are coming up the river, and it's not safe to keep the slaves here. They might rebel if they think the Yankees will help them."

"Hmph," Louvenia said. "Those boats had better take their time getting here. Missy Lafayette is giving a tea party this week, and I'll be right annoyed if she has to cancel it."

A tea party! Tennyson thought. *Soldiers and war are coming up the river, and she's talking about tea parties!*

"You shouldn't be going to *any* parties," said Julia. "You're still in mourning for your fiancé, in case you've forgotten."

"And by the way," Louvenia went on, ignoring Julia's last statement, "I'm deeply vexed that you hid away all of our jewels. What am I supposed to wear out? I'm going to look like a servant."

The sound of galloping hooves approached the house from outside. They thundered right up the stairs of the front porch and into the front hallway.

"Henry!" shouted Julia, shooting up out of her seat and upsetting the card table.

All three of them—Julia, Louvenia, and Tennyson—ran out into the hallway just in time to see young Henry Fontaine and his horse gallop out the back door at the far end of the Hall of Ancestors. He had literally ridden his horse straight through the house.

"Mother, do something," cried Louvenia. "This is the third time he's done that this week."

The sound of hooves approached the house again, this time from the back door, and Henry and his horse reappeared in the hallway.

"Hello, Mother," he said, bringing his heaving horse to a halt in front of Julia and Louvenia. The horse reared up and rolled its eyes when it saw Julia glaring at it.

"Take that horse outside," said Julia.

"I'm not going out until you let me join the army," Henry said.

"I won't let you do anything of the sort," Julia said. "You're only fourteen years old. Besides, you'll get to rule the roost now that your father is leaving and your three brothers are off fighting."

"I don't want to rule the roost; I want to fight. I hate being left here like a girl."

Atlas came into the hallway from outside.

"Not again, boy," he said when he saw Henry sitting there on his horse. And then, to Julia: "We're ready. Come and see us off."

They went out onto the front porch. Tennyson padded along after them and stopped in her tracks at the sight of hundreds of slaves walking down the oak alley, now shorn of the gold spiderweb canopy. At the end of the alley on the river bobbed several huge boats and the slaves were getting onto those boats.

"Take care of yourself, my beautiful wife," Atlas said to Julia.

"You don't have to worry about *me*," said Julia. "I'm more worried about *you*. Be very careful on the river. It makes me nervous that you're taking all the slaves at once."

Just then, there was a gasp behind them on the porch and Effie ran out onto the front lawn. She threw her arms around two young boys tagging along at the back of the line to the river.

"Please don't take my boys away with you," she cried.

"Effie!" shouted Julia. "Get back into the house this instant!"

"First you sell their father off last year and now you're sendin' my boys off too," Effie sobbed. "You're tearin' out my heart." Her boys started crying too.

"I told you to let go!" commanded Julia.

But Effie ignored her. Julia marched up to the slave, tore her away from her sons and threw her onto the ground. When Effie got up and ran toward her sons again, Julia hit her on the face, opening up Effie's nose. Blood spattered onto the white smashed-shell driveway. Tennyson screamed.

"When are you going to *listen* to me," Julia cried, her face red. "Get on that boat," she shouted at the boys, kicking the blood-covered shells at them.

"You really shouldn't have done that, Julia," Atlas said. "Leave it to the overseer next time."

"I know, Mother," said Louvenia, grimacing. "It makes you look so . . . manly."

Waves of horror and nausea smacked into Tennyson and then she heard herself shouting over and over again:

"What gives you the right? What gives you the right?"

But no one heard her and history happened anyway. Tennyson sat down and cried.

"Tennyson," said a voice, and she looked up in surprise. Who could see her there?

"Tennyson," said the voice again, and Tennyson realized

that she was halfway out of her dream by now and that the voice belonged to Hattie.

Then she wasn't on the front porch of Aigredoux at all, but on the moss bed, next to her little sister.

***

It was still the middle of the night.

"You were dreaming," said Hattie. "And shouting too."

Tennyson gripped the scratchy mattress and waited for the bad-dream feeling to flow out of her. But this time the sick feeling stayed right there inside her.

"Go back to sleep," she told Hattie after a minute. "I just want to get a little air." She slid off the bed.

The moonlight streamed in through the shutters. Tennyson looked out through the window and took several deep breaths. The sweet smell of night-blooming jasmine stained the air. Her dream anxiety ground itself down to a dull throb.

And then came a twinge of curiosity. This curiosity was about the vault beneath the stairs, whether it was real. Tennyson didn't see any reason to stand around and wonder about it when she could just go and see for herself.

When she got downstairs, Tennyson lit a candle in the dining room and took it into the Hall of Ancestors. She ran her hands over the grand staircase panels, just as Julia had done. After a few minutes her fingers found a tiny hole in the surface and her heart skipped a beat. Then she knelt down and felt along the cracks between the floorboards. Several splinters later, her finger felt metal and she picked a rusty knitting needle out of the floor.

The secret door swung open slowly, creaking on its hidden hinges, and decades of dust sighed out of the stairwell inside. Her heart pounded and her mouth tasted like rust, but Tennyson made herself go in and closed the panel behind her, careful to leave it open just the tiniest bit so she could get back out.

The stairs were damp and grimy and Tennyson went down very slowly. At the bottom of the stairs stood the dungeon-like door, just like in her dream, except the big lock was gone. Was the gold still inside, and that huge ivory trunk filled with priceless jewels? Tennyson took a deep breath and pulled on the door.

Empty.

The vault inside was empty. Tennyson sat down on the floor in front of the room, almost angry. Why had Aigredoux wanted her to know about this empty vault? She could understand if it had still been filled with the gold. Then she could have told Aunt Henrietta about it and the money would have saved everything. It would have saved Aigredoux from melting like sugar in the rain. It would have spared the house the humiliation of being stripped naked by workers to buy potatoes and candles and pay bills. It would have saved Tennyson and Hattie from Aunt Henrietta's idea about marrying them off to rich gentlemen callers when they were really just wild little girls who'd lived in the Mississippi woods their whole lives.

But instead the house had shown Tennyson an empty vault,

another reminder of what might have been, like Bon Vivant's columns.

Footsteps creaked thirty feet over Tennyson's head, up in the Hall of Ancestors.

"Who's there," called a voice.

Tennyson froze.

"I know there's someone there," said Zulma, her voice wavering. "I heard you walkin' round."

Tennyson hugged her knees to her chest, praying that the woman wouldn't notice the slightly ajar panel door. The footsteps padded around, and a few minutes later, Tennyson's modest prayer was answered. Then there was only the sound of her own breathing.

And then she realized that she'd been stupid, that she hadn't understood. The house hadn't given her an empty vault.

Not only had it given her a new dream to write into a story for Bartholomew Prentiss, it had given her a place to write about it without being discovered.

❖❖❖

Later that night, Tennyson brought her pen and the harp paper and the envelope with her magazines and letter and long green check down into the vault. As she got ready to write, in her mind she watched the boats disappearing up the river, carrying Atlas and the hundreds of Fontaine slaves away. And then she saw something else: Emery's truck disappearing back up the river road, being swallowed by the cane field.

So it wasn't the first time that it had fallen to the Fontaine women to protect Aigredoux and fend for themselves. This had happened over and over again. First Julia, then Aunt Henrietta, and now history wanted Tennyson and Hattie to be next in line.

It all comes down to you, Zulma had told her. *To keep the family goin' and Aigredoux standin'.*

It sent chills up Tennyson's spine, seeing how hard history tried to repeat itself.

Chapter Twelve
SAVING THE BACON

Several weeks later and over a thousand miles away, Bartholomew Prentiss sat at his usual table at Sardi's. He was just about
to take his first bite of his first lunchtime pork chop and wash it
down with his first sip of martini when he heard:

"Big Boy! Just who I wanted to see."

It was Mr. Nusselbaum, the owner of the magazine, and he
was holding a big bottle of champagne.

Bartholomew stood up warily, afraid that Mr. Nusselbaum
might hit him with the champagne bottle. After all, his boss had
never had a kind word to say to him before and right now he
looked a little wild around the eyes. But instead Mr. Nusselbaum
threw his arms around Bartholomew and gave his round middle
a squeeze.

"You did it!" he said, releasing the prisoner and uncorking the champagne, which fizzed over and spilled on Bartholomew's plate. "We usually print up ten thousand copies of our magazine. And now, thanks to that gothic Southern drama-orama you found, guess how many copies of the *Sophisticate* we had to print this week?"

"How many?" said Bartholomew, disdainfully shaking some champagne off his special red-velvet-lined cape.

"Half a million!" yelled Mr. Nusselbaum, taking a swig from the bottle and sitting down at the table. "It's a smash hit! A run-away success! And you and me, Big Boy—we're back in business!"

"While I am very glad that my discovery has been good for business," said Bartholomew loftily, "please know that I am first and foremost a Servant of Art. I believe that I may have uncovered the writer of the next great American novel, and that is all that matters to me."

"Whatever," said Mr. Nusselbaum. "You were this close to being a jobless slob before those stories came out. It's hard to be a Servant of Art when you're living in the gutter, wouldn't you say? This Fontaine chap sure saved your bacon." He lit a cigar. "I don't know why America's so crazy for this story. Guess they're tired of Little Orphan Annie and they want something juicier. Say, when do you think they're gonna get around to drawing some eyeballs on Annie anyway?" He laughed out a big cloud of cigar smoke.

Bartholomew coughed into a hanky. "Perhaps the American public simply knows good writing when they see it," he sniffed.

"That's giving 'em too much credit," said Mr. Nusselbaum. "But who cares. They love it. And I want the next story to go in next week's issue."

"I do not have the next story," said Bartholomew, nibbling daintily on an olive from his martini and wishing that Mr. Nusselbaum would go away.

"What? Why not?"

"Mr. Fontaine has not sent it to me yet," said Bartholomew. "I sent him a letter as soon as I received his last chapter and implored him to send the next installment. I imagine that he is writing it now and will send it when it is completed to his satisfaction."

"Who cares about *his* satisfaction?" roared Mr. Nusselbaum. "I want that story now. Get that man to sign a contract right away and sling some money in his direction. Give him a hundred bucks for starters. Then tell him you want a new chapter every two weeks and the whole book has to be published in the *Sophisticate*."

"Every two weeks!" exclaimed Bartholomew. "*Mr.* Nusselbaum. That is a very unreasonable demand. We are talking about *Art*, not a cheap toy on an assembly line!"

"We are *not* talking about art," thundered Mr. Nusselbaum. "We're talking about *money*. If there's money to be made, I'm going to make it. The public demands, and I supply. So get that next chapter and that contract or I'll send you out of the *Sophisticate* on a silver platter with an apple in your mouth."

When Mr. Nusselbaum put it this way, Bartholomew didn't see that he had much of a choice. He lumbered back to his office via the hot dog cart and hollered for Miss Goodenough.

"Yes, sir?" she said, wobbling into the clearing around his desk and carrying a big stuffed sack. "Oooph," she said as she dropped it on the floor.

"Heavens, what is that?" Bartholomew asked.

"Fan letters for Mr. Fontaine," explained Miss Goodenough. "What would you like me to do with them?"

"Don't just leave them here; take them away," said Bartholomew, hanging up his cape. "Did anything happen to come in the mail from Mr. Fontaine today?"

"I'm afraid not," said Miss Goodenough sadly.

"We need to get in touch with him," Bartholomew said. "To demand the next chapter and get him to agree to a contract."

"But we don't have his address," pointed out Miss Goodenough. "We only have a return address of the Ascension Parish Post Office, care of that fellow named Zipporah Tweed."

"Call the switchboard and see if they can locate a telephone number for a Fontaine residence in Ascension Parish."

Miss Goodenough went away and came back a few minutes later.

"If there's a Fontaine residence there, they don't have a telephone," she reported.

"So get the number for Zipporah Tweed at the post office," Bartholomew said.

"I tried that too," she said. "But the post office doesn't have a telephone either. It doesn't seem like there's . . . a whole lot around that area."

Bartholomew threw himself down in his chair. "We'll just have to send another letter then," he said. "And wait."

So they sent another letter and waited. They waited for one day, and then another, and soon seven working days had gone by. That amounted to twenty-one Sardi's pork chops and twenty-one Sardi's martinis, and still the next installment of Mr. Fontaine's novel did not turn up. More fan letters came in, and now people wondered when the next chapter would be published.

On the eighth day, Mr. Nusselbaum came into Bartholomew's office and paced in front of Bartholomew's desk with his tin pillbox.

"I got a call today from Hollywood," he said sweatily. "They want to make this book into a talkie, a moving film starring Pink Duveen. You know who she is?"

Bartholomew gripped the edge of his desk. "What?" he cried. Pink Duveen was a brassy blond actress who starred in gangster movies. She usually wore feather boas and fainted dramatically in every single scene. "That harlot is so dumb that she wouldn't know how to peel a potato. Who would she play in a moving film about *Aigredoux*?"

"They want her to play Louvenia Fontaine," said Mr. Nusselbaum. "Except they want to jazz up the character a little bit.

You know, make her a bit of a wisecracker. Have you had any luck getting the next chapter? Hollywood wants to know what happens next."

Bartholomew felt his lunch start to rise in his throat. "Not yet," he croaked. "We are trying everything we can to get in touch with Mr. Fontaine."

"You haven't tried everything," said Mr. Nusselbaum, popping a small handful of pills into his mouth. Then he called: "Miss Goodenough!"

"Yes, sir," she said, tottering through the paper alley.

"Book a round-trip ticket on a train to New Orleans," instructed Mr. Nusselbaum. "For tomorrow morning." And then, to Bartholomew: "Pack your bags. You're going down to Louisiana personally to meet with this Fontaine fellow. Once you get to New Orleans, hire a car and go over to Ascension Parish and find him."

"What?" cried Bartholomew. "Me?"

"Yes, you," said Mr. Nusselbaum. "Time's wasting, and time is money. Your job is to get the rest of his book and make him sign that contract. What's more, I want you to bring him back to New York with you so we can get him to write more stories for us. We're going to make him a star and get rich in the meantime. And if you come back empty-handed, don't bother to come back to this office."

When he left, Bartholomew and Miss Goodenough stared at each other in dismay.

"Oh, Miss Goodenough," Bartholomew said. "What have I done?"

"I'll go book your ticket, sir," she said.

Bartholomew scowled at the wall of manuscripts choking his desk and hated life. How dare Mr. Nusselbaum treat him like an errand boy! To send him off on a long inconvenient journey, just like that! And trains were *so* terribly uncomfortable, even in the first-class compartments—all of that jostling around. Furthermore, just think of all of the pork chops he would be missing! Bartholomew's stomach was very particular, and it was used to having three glazed pork chops a day. What if the dining car didn't serve glazed pork chops?

And how dare Mr. Nusselbaum treat the Fontaine novel so cheaply! Bartholomew hated being at the mercy of such a hamfisted man. But then again, he told himself, all great artists have had to suffer for their art. The tyranny of Mr. Nusselbaum and this tiresome journey were clearly a small price to pay to bring a great American novel into being. The whole country would thank him afterward.

"*Let us go then, you and I,*" he said, quoting his favorite T. S. Eliot poem to his special cape. "*Let us go and make our visit.*"

❖❖❖

It was still dark when Bartholomew arrived at Grand Central Station the next morning. Smoke and steam swirled around the train and the stationmaster blew on his whistle.

"All aboard," he called.

Bartholomew hustled down the platform, followed by a porter dragging a cart piled high with Bartholomew's six large alligator suitcases. One of those suitcases contained fan letters to this Tennyson chap, as a bribelike enticement to come to New York City.

Out of nowhere, a man stepped into Bartholomew's path and knocked him right onto the ground.

"Look where you're going, you buffoon!" cried Bartholomew over the hill of his stomach.

The porter helped Bartholomew up as the man rushed away and disappeared into the smoke and steam. "Some people ain't got no manners," he said as he helped heave Bartholomew and his luggage up into their first-class compartment.

Feeling rather sorry for himself, Bartholomew settled into a fine velvet armchair and covered himself with a nice fur blanket he'd brought along. Then he produced from his carry bag a thermos of tea, some bread, and a neat little jar of marmalade. Even though he was being forced to take this terribly inconvenient journey, he still liked to have everything just so. Bartholomew considered it his personal responsibility to set a civilized example. Once he'd eaten the bread and drunk the tea, he nestled down under his blanket and fell asleep.

"Sorry to wake you, sir," said a voice.

The lump under the fur blanket stirred and Bartholomew emerged blearily from beneath. "Are we there already?" he asked.

"No, sir, we're only in Newark, 'bout an hour outside the city," said the conductor. "I'm real sorry to wake you, but I need to see your ticket."

"Will these nuisances never end?" Bartholomew mumbled, and he reached into the inside pocket of his suit jacket. "That's funny," he said. "It was there this morning when I left my apartment."

He got up and dug around in all of his jacket pockets, but only lint came out. "My wallet's gone too," he added, waking up now. He turned his carry bag upside down, and out bounced four jars of marmalade, a loaf of bread, a tin of Harrods Earl Grey tea, and a little satin sleep mask. But no ticket and no wallet.

"Thief, thief!" cried Bartholomew. "Robber, thief! Someone has stolen my property! Oh, gods above—please tell me that they've spared my cape!"

The gods above had indeed spared his special cape, which still resided in the top alligator suitcase. But the fact remained that Bartholomew had no ticket and no money, and the manager had to be called.

"I know what happened," cried Bartholomew, who had retreated back to the soothing safety of his fur blanket. "That man on the platform intentionally bumped into me, and while I was lying there, injured, he made off with my wallet and ticket. Turn this train around at once so we can apprehend the criminal."

The manager and the conductor looked at each other.

"I'm afraid that it's rather impossible to turn the train

around, sir," said the manager. "And I'm afraid that since you have no ticket, you will have to move out of our first-class accommodation."

"What!" shrieked Bartholomew. "Where am I to go?"

"Well, you have no ticket and no money to buy a ticket," explained the manager apologetically. "I'm afraid that you will have to get off at the next stop, in Philadelphia."

"But I am on an extremely important mission in Louisiana!" Bartholomew informed him, shaking his blanket indignantly. "I must get to New Orleans right away."

"I'm sorry, sir, but those are the rules."

The conductor lingered after the manager left.

"Why are you still here persecuting me?" said Bartholomew miserably. "You'll be rid of me soon enough."

"Look," said the conductor. "I feel real bad for you. If you don't tell no one, I can put you on another part of the train. It ain't fancy like this, but it'll get you to New Orleans."

"Oh?" said Bartholomew. "Really! I would be most grateful."

"Meet me on the platform in Philly."

Two hours later, Bartholomew lugged his six suitcases and his carry bag of marmalade onto the Philadelphia platform and waited.

"It's all the way at the back of the train," said the conductor when he found Bartholomew, and they dragged his alligator cases to the end of the platform.

"But this is a *livestock* car," said Bartholomew, recoiling.

"Yeah, but it's almost empty, so you're in luck," said the conductor. "There's only a few chicken coops. The rest is all straw, so you can make a nice bed for yourself."

"Oh, the horror," blanched Bartholomew as the smell of chicken droppings wafted past him.

The train whistle blew.

"You gettin' on or not?" asked the conductor impatiently.

Time's wasting, and time is money, said Mr. Nusselbaum's voice in the back of Bartholomew's mind. *If you come back empty-handed, don't bother to come back to this office.*

Bartholomew nodded. He started to climb into the car and the conductor shoved his big behind until he made it. Bartholomew covered his nose with his fur blanket and the conductor threw his precious alligator bags into the filthy straw.

"Thank you," Bartholomew forced himself to say.

"That's all right," said the conductor. "These are tough times. All of us can use a break now and then. Lay low now, and good luck in New Orleans."

Then he slid the door shut, sealing Bartholomew inside with his cape, jars of jam, and three dozen squawking chickens.

And thus began the journey of Bartholomew Prentiss.

Chapter Thirteen

RED MORNING

She felt very peculiar and it took a minute for Tennyson to figure out that the bed was rocking beneath her. Like a swing or a cradle—a long, slow movement in one direction and then back again. She opened her eyes.

"You must have nodded off," Emery said, sitting in the far end of their rowboat. "You've missed all the good fish. It's almost dawn."

Tennyson sat up. Overhead the stars were disappearing, but the pale moon still shone down on them. Innisfree stood in the distance, on a forested bluff overlooking the river.

"How did I get here?" she asked. "When did you come back?"

"Tennyson—look!" cried Hattie, pointing at a fat silver fish in the bottom of the boat. It was still alive, its eyes wide and gills still moving. "I caught it! Papa helped me—but just a little bit."

"We'll cook it up and surprise your mother with it for breakfast," said Emery, reeling in a line.

"Is she back?" asked Tennyson. *Don't let yourself believe this,* she thought. *It has to be a dream.* But her heart fought her mind and she could feel herself believing it. The strange familiarity wrapped itself around her like a blanket and soothed her into believing it. Her fight softened and broke down and tears of relief blurred her eyes.

"You're so strange right now," said Hattie, looking at her. "Back from where? Mama's at home, sleeping. You know she never comes night fishing with us."

Water lapped against the sides of the boat and it made a slow, tranquil circle in the river.

"Well, would you look at that," said Emery, staring at the horizon. "It's going to be a red sunrise. That's a bad omen."

"What do you mean?" asked Hattie.

"It's an old sailor's saying," Emery told her. *"Red at night, sailor's delight. Red in the morning, sailors take warning."* He pulled up the anchor. "Let's go home."

The girls huddled in the bottom of the boat together. Hattie poured water on the fat silver fish.

"Why did you do that?" Tennyson asked.

"To make him feel better," Hattie explained.

"It will just keep him alive longer," Tennyson said. "That's cruel."

The sky on the horizon burned pink as the red sun got ready to rise. Tennyson looked up at her father. He was starting to fade as the sky got lighter and Tennyson hated herself for getting tricked by another dream.

"No," she cried out to Emery. "Don't leave again." But soon he faded away to nothing and the girls were alone in the boat.

"Don't cry, Tennyson," said Hattie, alarmed. Tennyson rarely cried. But she was crying now, in that deep bitter way you cry when your hopes have been raised and smashed.

Tennyson leaned over the edge of the boat and her tears fell into the river, making big salty rings in the surface. Then the red sun rose and she could see down to the river bottom and there were the little girls. They turned their white faces up and their dark sad eyes stared at Tennyson. Then the last downturned face looked up at her.

It was Sadie.

Before she knew what was happening, Tennyson was in the water too, falling down, down to the silty bottom.

And then she woke up.

✦✦✦

Hattie was already up, standing by the window.

"Tennyson," she said. "The sun's so funny today."

Tennyson sat up. "What do you mean?"

"Look for yourself."

A heavy red-dawn sun throbbed over the cane fields. So Tennyson hadn't been dreaming her own dream after all. Now she was seeing what would happen next, as well as what had already happened.

"Why is it red?" asked Hattie.

"Maybe it just feels like it," said Tennyson, not telling Hattie about her dream.

Red in the morning, sailors take warning.

After breakfast there were blue letters to mail, and one from Uncle Twigs too. By then the sun wasn't red anymore but everything still felt strange outside. No breeze blew off the river. Nothing moved, not a single leaf. It felt like everything was holding its breath and waiting for something to happen.

"Mr. Tweed, are you there?" called Tennyson as she ran up the stairs to the post office.

He was there, standing in front of the window and stroking his beard.

"I didn't think you were here," Tennyson said. "I didn't smell your pipe." She put down the letters and joined him at the window. "It's strange outside today."

"Yes, it is," said Zipporah. "I haven't seen weather like this for a long time."

"Maybe a storm is coming," suggested Tennyson.

"I don't think so," Zipporah said. "My grandmama used to say that when things stood real still like this, God was tryin' to make his mind up 'bout somethin'."

Tennyson didn't like the sound of this. There were too many undecided fates in her life, and she didn't want God to make up his mind about them on a day when the sun had risen red.

Zipporah saw the look on her face. "Oh, you don't need to worry," he assured her. "Your plan's still workin'. I got a couple of letters for you here, from that fellow at the *Sophisticate*. He wants more chapters right away. You're gettin' to be a big star."

He held up a new issue of the *Sophisticate* and showed her the page with her latest chapter:

"Before the Storm"
By Tennyson Fontaine

> *This is the second chapter of a serial. Due to popular demand, the* Sophisticate *will be publishing the work in its entirety. Look for the next chapter in a future issue.*

"And another ten dollars too," said Zipporah. "You're gonna be rich soon."

Tennyson took the check. She felt bad about having money when Aunt Henrietta was struggling. But there was no way to give Aunt Henrietta the money without telling her about the stories. So that was that. The checks were just decoration, pretty sheets of green paper.

"Don't go yet," Zipporah said. "I've got some mail for your aunt and uncle too." He handed her two envelopes. "They look important, so be careful with 'em."

Tennyson tucked all of the letters inside her dress and walked back past the statue-still bone forests.

To her surprise, a man stood on the river road, in front of the gnarled lazy-oak alley leading up to Aigredoux. In front of him stood a camera on a tripod.

"Who are you?" asked Tennyson.

"I'm with the WPA," he said distractedly.

"The what?"

"The Works Progress Administration," he answered. "It's part of the government."

"Why are you taking a picture of Aigredoux?" asked Tennyson warily.

"It's my job," he said. "We're supposed to take pictures of all the old houses around here before they fall down. From the looks of this one, I got here just in time, eh?"

Tennyson didn't say anything.

The man lit a cigarette. "There's something funny about this place, though," he said, exhaling.

"What do you mean?"

"Well, every time I try to take a picture of it, my camera jams. It's creepy. Bet you're glad you don't live here, huh, kid?"

"I do live here," said Tennyson, and she ran up the alley. The ghost moss hung low from the trees, protecting the house from the gaze of the man's camera. Tennyson wanted to protect the house too, and when she got inside, she called for Zulma.

"Why're you shriekin' like that?" said Zulma, coming down

the Hall of Ancestors and wiping her hands on a rag. "Sounds like you're tryin' to raise the dead."

"There's a strange man outside taking pictures of Aigredoux," Tennyson reported.

"Is that so," said Zulma, marching out of the house. When she got to the end of the oak alley, she made short work of the man from the WPA, and soon he went away with his broken camera.

"People're gettin' ruder every day," Zulma muttered darkly, slamming the front door behind her. "That man'll be lucky if he don't get shot, doin' that. It'll remind people round here of that snake, Colonel Tillman."

"Who?"

"Colonel Gabriel Tillman," said Zulma, looking through the shuttered front window to make sure the man was gone. "He was a Yankee colonel, in charge of the gunboats that came up the river durin' the war. That man rained death round here, blowin' up houses left and right. And he was real sinister 'bout it too. First he'd take a picture of a house, and then he'd stick the dynamite in. Give folks a few minutes to save what they could and get out. They say he used to carry round a whole photograph album of houses he burned down, just to show it off."

She looked down at Tennyson. "What've you got there?"

"A letter for Aunt Henrietta and one for Uncle Twigs too."

"Lord have mercy," cried Zulma when she saw the one for Aunt Henrietta. "It's from Washington, D.C." She clutched the letter to her heart and paced back and forth, her eyes closed and her lips moving.

"What's the matter?" asked Tennyson.

"Don't you understand?" hissed Zulma. "All those letters she's been sendin' off, and her mother, and her grandmother, tryin' to get the Fontaines' fortune back from the government. They've been waitin' *five whole generations* for an answer and this might be it. Get down on your knees and say a prayer, quick."

"But I've never said a prayer before." Tennyson wavered. "What do I say?"

"What?" screamed Zulma. "Never said a prayer? What kind of a godless house was Mister Emery runnin' out there in the woods, voodoo girl?"

The door to the ladies' parlor opened.

"What's going on?" asked Aunt Henrietta.

"Scram," said Zulma to Tennyson, and then she disappeared into the parlor with Aunt Henrietta and shut the door.

All of the clocks in the house stopped ticking and the people in the portraits hanging on the walls held their breath. The world came to a standstill as Aunt Henrietta opened her letter from Washington, the answer to five generations of pleading on thousands of sheets of thin blue paper.

A sound came from the ladies' parlor, not a sound that Tennyson had heard before. Then it got louder and even louder and it made the hair on the back of Tennyson's neck rise. Suddenly she pictured Jos with his leg caught and shredded in a bear trap and she imagined that was the sort of sound he would make.

"What's that noise?" asked Hattie, running down the grand staircase. Uncle Twigs appeared at the door of the gentlemen's parlor.

"I don't know," whispered Tennyson. "I think it's Aunt Henrietta."

Uncle Twigs ran across the hallway to the ladies' parlor and slid the door open, and inside Tennyson saw Aunt Henrietta clutching the open letter and bawling with her mouth open. Then she buried her face in Zulma's stomach and Zulma wrapped her arms around Aunt Henrietta's head. The sight made Tennyson feel queasy, especially when she thought that if this had been a hundred years earlier, Zulma would have been Aunt Henrietta's slave and that the money in question was made from the blood of Zulma's ancestors who were buried out in the yard and not hanging in portraits in the Hall of Ancestors and that despite all of this, Aunt Henrietta was still willing to ask for Zulma's comfort on a day like this. Tennyson couldn't look anymore, and she turned and ran through the hallways until she reached the kitchen. There she crawled under the table like a child and sat there, her knees pulled up to her chest.

Soon Hattie's legs came into view and her little face appeared under the table.

"What're you doing under there?" she asked. "What's going on?"

"Aunt Henrietta just got a letter from the government, telling her that she's not getting any money back," Tennyson told her. "Aigredoux's done for."

Hattie crawled under the table and sat just like Tennyson, except she put her head on Tennyson's shoulder.

"Do you think Mama and Papa would be glad?" Hattie asked. "They always said that the money was tainted."

The faint sound of Aunt Henrietta's sobs echoed down the hallways.

"I don't think they'd be glad," said Tennyson. "I don't think they'd know how to feel."

And she realized that that's probably why Emery left Aigredoux in the first place. All of the love and hate and despair of the place was too overwhelming, too much to figure out. And you drank it all in until it was like a strange poison-like candy that stayed in your blood.

Aigredoux. Bittersweet.

A red morning, indeed.

❖❖❖

Because all bad things happen in threes, two more bad things happened that day. First of all, workers came and took the last of the marble covering the stairs, and they were so rough that they tore up one of the stairs entirely, leaving a gaping hole in the staircase. Then Uncle Twigs went into the gentlemen's parlor and opened *his* letter and was informed that he was no longer the president of the Louisiana Society for the Strict Enforcement of the Proper Use of the English Language. The other three members had taken a vote and the presidency was now in the hands of a man named Edgar Jefferson Addison Wentworth IV.

So everyone in the house, including the house itself, had been bruised and insulted and humiliated—except for Tennyson, who'd gotten good news on the red-sun morning. She lay low and guarded this good news with her life even after the sun went down, in case God was still making up his mind about things.

Chapter Fourteen

EYE FOR AN EYE

Zulma shook Tennyson awake in the middle of the night.

"Get up," she said, the yellow light from her oil lamp bouncing around on the walls. "You've got to take the letters to the post office."

"What?" said Tennyson groggily. "What letters?"

"These," said Zulma, handing her a stack of tissue-thin blue letters.

"Why did Aunt Henrietta write more letters?" asked Tennyson. "I thought the government said no about giving her the Fontaine money back."

"Quit your sassin' and go," said Zulma.

Still confused, Tennyson got up and left the house with the letters. As she stumbled along the river road, the sky grew lighter.

A wind came off the river and blew the feather-light letters all over the road. She scrambled around, snatching them up.

Footsteps echoed from around the bend and suddenly a young boy ran past her.

"Hurry up," he shouted. "We're going to miss it."

"Miss what?" asked Tennyson, but the boy ignored her.

Another young boy appeared around the bend, panting. "I don't know why you're runnin'," he said. "It'll never happen. The Yankees won't dare blow up Bon Vivant."

"That's what you think," said the first boy. "They said it was going to happen at dawn, and it's already gettin' light. So keep runnin'."

Bon Vivant? puzzled Tennyson. *But the only thing left of Bon Vivant is those columns, the ones God left as a reminder.*

Then she looked down at her hands and saw that the blue letters had disappeared like steam into the air. So she knew that once again she was in a dream and she ran after the boys down the river road.

Soon they got to the place where the bones of Bon Vivant stood, the columns covered in dying vines that looked like tendrils of long black hair. But on this morning, in this dream, a magnificent white house stood there instead. It was almost as magnificent as Aigredoux. Even though the sun hadn't yet risen, a crowd of people huddled on the lawn, their faces filled with worry and anguish.

All of a sudden, soldiers came out of the house and pushed the crowd away from it.

"Get back, get back!"

An older soldier walked down the front stairs of the magnificent house and stood in front of the people gathered on the lawn. He was clearly in charge.

"Let the destruction of Bon Vivant be an example to all traitors to the Union," he shouted. Then he faced the house and yelled: "Everyone out."

The family and slaves who lived inside Bon Vivant poured out of the house, lugging candlesticks and paintings and chairs, whatever they could carry. Then some of the soldiers went inside and carried out a woman, who kicked and screamed and scratched at them.

"Poor Elizabeth," whispered one of the women in the crowd. "Her father built Bon Vivant. It's going to kill her to see it demolished."

Then the house was empty, and the family stood in despair next to their pile of chairs and candlesticks and paintings. A soldier called out from the porch,

"Now, Colonel Tillman?"

It'll remind people round here of that snake, Colonel Tillman.

Who?

Colonel Gabriel Tillman. That man rained death round here.

Tennyson moved closer to get a look at him. Colonel Tillman didn't look like a man who rained death. He looked earnest, like a doctor, and this somehow made him even scarier. Being near him made the hair stand up on the back of Tennyson's neck.

"The dynamite's inside," the soldier said.

"Don't blow it yet," said the colonel. He whistled and one of the soldiers marched through the crowd with something that looked like an accordion on sticks. The colonel set it up on the lawn and faced it toward the house. He disappeared under a blanket attached to the accordion and Tennyson realized that it was an old camera.

"The light's not strong enough yet," the colonel announced, emerging from underneath. "We'll have to wait."

The family of Bon Vivant clung to each other and wept. Colonel Tillman and his soldiers lit cigars and sat down. One of the soldiers went inside and came back out with fine crystal glasses and a goblet of wine, and the soldiers drank it and waited for the sun to rise.

"Watch this," said a soldier, and he threw a crystal glass in the air and shot it with his pistol. "Target practice."

This set off a crystal-shooting contest.

Soon the sun rose over the fields and the crystal glasses glinted as they were thrown into the air. Colonel Tillman disappeared under the camera blanket again and stayed there for a long time. When he emerged again, he looked very happy and he said, "Now."

The soldiers ran at the crowd. "Clear out!" they cried again and again until everyone was standing on the other side of the river road. Two soldiers went inside with torches, and when they came out, black smoke billowed out of Bon Vivant's windows and doors. Everyone in the crowd started coughing and choking but no one left. Suddenly there was an explosion from deep inside the house, and glass and wood blew across the lawn. Flames soared out of the windows and there was a terrible tremor. Bon Vivant staggered and bowed and then finally crumbled into a blazing heap. Only the charred columns remained. A hush fell over the crowd and all of the men took off their hats.

Colonel Tillman stood with his soldiers, admiring the smoldering ruin.

"At least we'll always have the memories, won't we, gentlemen," he said, and they all laughed. "Let's move up the river." They pushed through the crowd down to the river landing and got back into their gunboats.

Up the river, thought Tennyson. *That means Aigredoux.*

She began to run.

✦✦✦

The boats were already anchored in front of the house when Tennyson got there. Soldiers sat up against the lazy trees of the oak alley, their rifles and swords propped up next to them. Others stood around on the path and kicked at the white smashed shells.

Several peacocks bumbled across the lawn, coming to investigate the commotion.

"Watch this," said one soldier to another, picking up his rifle. He aimed at one of the peacocks and fired. "Target practice."

"Good shot," said the other soldier. "Let's take its feathers."

"Souvenirs."

Tennyson's stomach clenched and she ran up the shell drive and into the house.

Soldiers stood around the now-empty Hall of Ancestors, their boots making muddy tracks on the white marble floor. The door to the gentlemen's parlor stood open, and a familiar voice came from inside:

"This document is an oath of loyalty to the Union. If you sign it, we won't take any offensive action against you. We will requisition some supplies from your property, but it will be exempt from torching and dynamiting, that sort of thing."

Tennyson looked into the room as Colonel Gabriel Tillman leaned back in a chair, having just finished his little speech. He was still smoking the cigar he'd lit at Bon Vivant.

Julia sat in a chair across from him.

"Your terms are very generous," she said, stony-faced.

"The age of chivalry isn't over yet," said the colonel, smiling around his cigar.

Julia stood up and looked out the front window at the soldiers in the oak alley. A shot sounded and a peacock screamed until another shot silenced it.

"Colonel Tillman," she said. "My highest priority is to preserve Aigredoux. I'll sign anything to get you off my property."

"So, you'll turn your back on the glorious Southern cause, just like that? Be a traitor to your neighbors and your whole way of life? That was easy."

"I'm a traitor any way you look at it, Colonel," said Julia. "If

I say no to you, you'll call me a traitor to the United States and burn my home to the ground. And if I agree to sign, I'm a traitor to the South. Since I'm damned either way, I have to act out of sheer self-interest." She took the oath from him and signed it on a desk, the desk that Uncle Twigs would use some seven decades later.

"Besides," she added, handing the paper to the colonel. "This war has been bad for business."

"By God, Southern women are hard," said the colonel, standing up and taking the document.

"Get out."

The colonel marched out into the hallway. "Take everything," he told his soldiers.

"What?" cried Julia. "You said that you would just take supplies."

"You just signed an oath to us," said the colonel. " 'Supplies' is a broad category, and you are now obligated to give us whatever support we demand."

Outside, soldiers led the Fontaines' horses around from the stables behind the house. Then they herded the pigs and even the chickens onto the front lawn until the barns were empty. They set the dovecotes on fire and the doves that didn't escape screamed. Crashes sounded all over the house as soldiers took furniture, mirrors, curtains—and even nails from the walls. A soldier dragged Louvenia's harp halfway out of the ladies' parlor.

"What in Sam Hill—" said Colonel Tillman. "What're you going to do with a harp, for God's sake? Leave it."

"All right," said the soldier, and dropped it with a horrible *twang* onto the ground.

Louvenia, still in her mourning dress, and all of the house servants ran to the gentlemen's parlor. They huddled behind Julia and helplessly watched the carnage.

"Are there any men of military age here?" the colonel asked Julia.

"No," Julia said. "My husband and all of my sons are off fighting."

What about Henry? wondered Tennyson, remembering the young son who'd been riding his horse through the house, the one who'd been left behind. *He must be hiding.*

"Colonel," reported a soldier. "We haven't recovered any silver or jewelry or that sort of thing."

"Where's all the silver?" the colonel asked Julia. "Surely a house this well appointed wouldn't be without."

"Stolen," Julia lied. "You aren't the first Yankee marauders to come up the river."

The soldiers pillaged the house until they were tired of carrying out all of the souvenirs. Then they smashed up the statues of the Greek gods outside. When that was done, they chopped up the furniture on the front lawns to make fires and roast the pigs and chickens they had killed.

Julia watched with iron composure.

"You've taken everything we have," she said to the colonel. "Can you please get out of my house now?"

"Thank you again for your hospitality, Mrs.—" Colonel

Tillman glanced down at the name on the oath. "Mrs. Fontaine." He bowed and cheerfully turned to leave.

"Wait," said a voice from the back of the gentlemen's parlor.

The colonel stopped and everyone turned around.

"You ain't got everythin' yet," Effie said.

Julia's face went chalk white. "What are you talking about, Effie?" she croaked, staring daggers at her slave.

Effie swept right past her. "Wait till you see this," she said to the colonel as she marched over to the paneled side of the grand staircase. Then she knelt on the ground and pulled the knitting needle out from between the floorboards.

"What are you doing?" screamed Julia. She lunged toward Effie, but two soldiers grabbed her arms and held her back.

The secret door opened easily and the soldiers streamed down the hidden stairs. A minute later, they heard metal pounding against metal. They were smashing the lock on the vault door.

"Holy Mary, mother of God," one of them cried from thirty feet below, and soon they emerged with Julia's ivory box of priceless jewels.

"This one's as big as a peach pit," said one of them, holding up a ruby. Another soldier took out a diamond tiara and put it on his head as they carried the box outside, hooting with disbelief and joy.

Then came the bars of gold, one by one. Up the stairs and out the door amidst jubilant cries from the soldiers carrying them.

"That's not all we found, sir," called a soldier from the stair-well. "Look at this." And he emerged, pulling Henry out of the darkness.

Colonel Tillman stared at Julia and shook his head.

"Jezebel," he said. "Liar. I told you to declare all men of mili-tary age." He turned to his soldiers. "Take him away," he or-dered, and the soldiers grabbed Henry and marched him down the front stairs.

"No!" screamed Julia. "He's just a boy! He's just a little boy!"

Henry cried and tried to break free, but the soldiers carted him down the oak alley toward the gunboats. Julia turned her wrath in Effie's direction. She probably would have torn the slave to shreds, but the Yankee soldiers still held her arms.

"How could you?" she screamed, the veins in her neck and her eyes bulging. "You poisonous snake! After everything we've done for you—fed you, clothed you, catered to your every need. We are your *family*. How could you betray us?"

Effie calmly took off her apron and dropped it on the floor. She walked over to Julia and stared into her face.

"You took my sons," she said. "An eye for an eye."

Then she spat at Julia's feet and walked out the front door.

✦✦✦

Then it was evening. The gunboats had gone.

Tennyson trailed after Julia and Louvenia as they walked over the grounds. Pig carcasses and chicken bones and dead peacocks littered the lawn. Burning piles of bedsteads and tables and chairs and armoires still smoldered on the grass. All of the gardens had been torn up, and shredded petals mixed with the smoke and ashes in the air.

In the middle of the smashed-shell path stood a chair that for some reason had escaped the ax, a lovely bedroom chair with a velvet cushion. Julia sat down wearily.

Louvenia stood next to her and cried.

"We might as well be dead," she sobbed. "It's all over."

"Nothing's over," said Julia.

"What are you talking about?" sobbed Louvenia. "They took Henry. We have nothing. No servants, no money, nothing to eat. They even tore up the vegetable gardens. This is the end."

Julia smiled grimly. "No, my darling, it's not," she said. "We'll feel the pain of this day for generations. This is only the beginning of our ruin."

Tennyson looked up at the house and saw that it had lost its color. The blinding white Aigredoux of her dreams had become the colorless temple of her reality.

Just like that.

❖❖❖

When Tennyson opened her eyes and was certain she was out of her dream, she slipped out of bed and went straight down the stairs and opened the hidden panel.

In the secret vault in the earth, she lit a candle and sat

crossed-legged on the floor. She imagined how terrible it must have been for young Henry Fontaine to cower down here while the soldiers ransacked his family's house above. And how sickening it must have been when the secret door opened and the light coursed down the stairs and the soldiers came down to take him away.

She picked up her mother's pen and wrote down her dream. The harp paper was growing moldy from being stored in the dank vault, but Tennyson hoped that Bartholomew Prentiss wouldn't hold it against her.

Footsteps creaked on the floor above.

"Who's there," called Zulma. "I know someone's there, down beneath the stairs. I see the candlelight and I can smell the match."

Tennyson's heart stopped. How could Zulma see the candlelight? And then she remembered: the workers had torn off a stair in the grand staircase. So now Zulma could see into the cavern below. Tennyson blew out the candle and huddled in the dark.

Zulma paced around the staircase above.

"I'm comin' in there," she called, "if I have to go through that broken stair."

Tennyson heard Zulma knock on the paneled side, looking for a way in.

Please don't open, please don't open, she thought, and prayed that she'd closed the panel tightly enough.

But she hadn't closed it tightly enough and the secret door

did open when Zulma pressed on it. Her oil lamp shone into the secret stairwell and soon she followed the light down the stairs.

"*You!*" she hissed at Tennyson. "What are you—how did you—?" She was so overwhelmed that she couldn't even get words out.

"I didn't do anything wrong," said Tennyson, squinting in the light.

"What is this place?" Zulma cried. "And how'd you know 'bout it? I lived here my whole life and never knew 'bout any secret stairs."

"I dreamed about it," said Tennyson, terrified to tell Zulma anything more.

"Oh, you *dreamed* about it, did you, voodoo girl?" said Zulma. "More likely you were snoopin' through Miz Henrietta's private papers and read 'bout it somehow. And what's all this?" She snatched up a page of Tennyson's writing.

"It's just a story I'm writing, for myself," Tennyson lied, but then Zulma spotted one of the *Sophisticate* issues on the ground. Both of them lunged for it at the same time but Zulma was bigger so she won.

" '*The Tragedy of Louvenia Fontaine,* by Tennyson Fontaine,' " she read, and her lips moved as she scanned the page. She looked up at Tennyson in horror.

"I can explain," Tennyson cried, but before she could say another word Zulma stuck the corner of the magazine into her oil lamp, and when it caught on fire, she dropped it onto the pile of harp paper. The brittle pages and even the envelope with the green checks went up in flames and Tennyson let out a scream. She tried to stamp out the fire but it was too late and soon all the papers were ashes.

Zulma's face glowed in the light.

"You demon!" she hissed, glaring down at Tennyson. "Miz Henrietta would up and *die* if she knew you were airin' this family's misfortunes and dirty laundry in a magazine. And you *knew* that, or else you wouldn't be hidin' down here like a criminal. You tell one word to Miz Henrietta 'bout what you've been doin', and boy, will you be sorry. She's in enough pain as it is without you stabbin' her in the back with the biggest knife you could find."

It's all over. This is the end.

Louvenia's words echoed in Tennyson's ears as helpless rage burned in her throat. But there was nothing in the world she could do. And so this was the end.

❖❖❖

So, now everyone was a traitor. Zulma was a traitor to Tennyson. Tennyson was a traitor to Aunt Henrietta. Sadie was a traitor to her whole family. Julia and Effie were traitors to each other.

Since they were all damned any way you looked at it, they all acted out of sheer self-interest.

It was just another one of those things that they handed down to each other, through the generations.

Chapter Fifteen

DAISY

The taxi driver nodded asleep, and his head fell forward and hit the steering wheel.

"Ugh," he groaned, and rolled down his window. "Hey, kid, c'mere," he shouted to one of the shoeshine boys waiting outside the New Orleans train station.

"Yeah?"

The taxi driver gave him a nickel. "Go get me a cup of coffee, will ya?" he said. "I worked all night and I can't keep my eyes open. You can keep the change for yourself."

He rolled up the window again and turned on the car radio. Then he closed his eyes while he listened to the music and soon he drifted off again.

They used to tell me I was building a dream,
 and so I followed the mob,
When there was earth to plow, or guns to
 bear,
I was always there right on the job.
They used to tell me I was building a dream,
 with peace and glory ahead,
Why should I be standing in line, just
 waiting for bread?
Brother, can you spare a dime?

Someone rapped on his window and the driver jerked awake.

"Took you long enough—" he started to say but stopped midsentence. It wasn't the shoeshine boy but rather a strange-looking round man in a red-velvet-lined cape. Chicken feathers stuck out of his hair and he carried a single alligator suitcase.

"Good morning," said Bartholomew grandly. "I need you to ferry me to Ascension Parish."

"Whoa, there," said the taxi driver. "That's three hours outside the city, maybe four, depending on where you're goin'. You got the dough?"

"Of course I do," scoffed Bartholomew. "Look at this fine cape and bag. Are these the adornments of a pauper?"

"All right, then," said the driver suspiciously. "Hop in."

"There is one negligible problem, however," admitted Bartholomew. "I don't actually have the money on my person."

"Huh?"

"I was robbed in New York City," explained Bartholomew. "But don't worry, my good fellow. I am Bartholomew Prentiss of the *Sophisticate* magazine, with which you are undoubtedly familiar. And if you give me your name and address, I shall post you the fare when I return to New York."

"Hold it right there, fatty," said the driver. "No money, no ride." He turned the key in the ignition.

"Please!" pleaded Bartholomew. "I've been crammed into a livestock car for three whole days! As if that wasn't bad enough, someone crept in and stole my luggage while we were stopped in Atlanta. They even stole my fur blanket! All I have left is this sole bag. Have a heart!"

"Sorry," said the driver. "A man's gotta think with his stomach these days, not his heart. If I don't get paid, I don't eat." And he rolled up his window and drove away.

"Ohhh," wailed Bartholomew. His unhappy stomach growled at the mention of eating, for he'd been subsisting on his jars of marmalade. He picked up his only remaining suitcase, stuffed with inedible fan letters, and set out to rummage up something to eat.

Soon the smell of cooking led him into a market square. In the corner of the square stood a gumbo stall. Several workers sat around the stall on crates, eating from steaming bowls.

"Oh, heavenly gumbo," said Bartholomew. "Ambrosia of the gods." And then, to the owner of the stall: "How much is a bowl?"

The stall owner eyed Bartholomew's special cape and alligator case.

"Ten dollars," he said. The workers on the crates laughed and kept eating.

The smell nearly drove Bartholomew wild with hunger. He reached into the breast pocket of his suit and produced a gold Cartier pocket watch on a chain.

"I'll trade you this gold watch for an unlimited amount of gumbo," he said, practically drooling.

The stall owner grabbed the watch and examined it.

"Is this real?" he asked.

"Of course it is," said Bartholomew. "Mr. Cartier made it for me himself."

"You got yourself a deal," said the gumbo man.

Bartholomew rubbed his hands together and sat down on his suitcase. Six bowls of gumbo later, his stomach was almost full but he still had a big problem.

"I need to get to Ascension Parish," he said to the workers, who had been watching his gumbo-consuming activities in awe.

"You got another gold watch?" asked one of them.

"I'm afraid I do not," said Bartholomew woefully.

"Why's a fancy fella like you goin' up there anyway?" asked another.

"I have very important business to attend to there," Bartholomew said secretively, and ran his finger along the inside of his bowl. "Is there any gumbo left?"

"You ate it all," said the stall owner, clapping the cover down on top of the pot.

A stringy barefooted boy stood up. His face was as tan as

leather and he looked about fourteen years old. "I'm goin' up that way, up the river road. I can take you."

"Thank you, my fine boy!" Bartholomew exclaimed, lurching up off his crate. "And I will be happy to furnish you with the appropriate payment as soon as I get back to New York. Kindly write down your address for me."

"Don't know how to write," said the boy. "And I don't have no address."

"What do you mean, you have no address?"

"I live over at Monk Swamp. Just a bunch of shacks there. They ain't got addresses."

"Oh, that rather does present a problem, doesn't it," said Bartholomew.

"Tell you what," said the boy. "I'll trade you a ride for that cape."

Bartholomew leaped back as though a snake had bitten his toe.

"Oh, I couldn't!" he cried, drawing the velvet protectively around his gumbo-filled belly. "My dear, beloved cape!"

"Suit yourself," said the boy, turning to leave.

Suddenly Mr. Nusselbaum's peevish face appeared in Bartholomew's mind like a black thundercloud.

"Listen to me, Big Boy," the thundercloud said, lightning sparking out on all sides. "If you don't hand over that ridiculous cape and get into that wagon with the swamp boy, I'm gonna turn your office into a janitor's closet."

"Wait," Bartholomew called to the boy, and in despair he handed over the cape. He watched miserably as the dirty boy from Monk Swamp tied it around his neck and modeled it for the other workers.

"Follow me," he said, and he led Bartholomew to a donkey-drawn wagon filled with splintery wood and smelly barrels. "You can ride in back."

"What's in the barrels?" Bartholomew asked, covering his nose and mouth with a hanky.

"Sardines," said the boy. "I was sellin' 'em in the square. When you dry 'em out, they make good crawfish bait."

And they rolled out of the city: Bartholomew Prentiss, Servant of Art, hunkered down between two barrels of sardines, and the swamp boy sitting up front, proudly wearing his new red-velvet-lined cape. It was not a sight that you see very frequently. But then again, they were in New Orleans, where anything could happen and often did.

So no one looked twice.

❖❖❖

Soon they were out of the city and the wagon bumped along the river road. The noon sun beat down on them, and Bartholomew took off his suit jacket and vest and fanned himself with his hanky. The swamp boy took off his shirt too, but then he tied the velvet cape back on anyway.

"You up there," called Bartholomew. "What is your name?"

"Daisy."

"That's your *name*?"

"Uh-huh."

"How curious," said Bartholomew. "Why did your parents name a boy Daisy?"

"I dunno."

"My, aren't you a lively conversationalist," said Bartholomew. "What do you do for a living, Daisy?"

"I'm a driftwooder," said Daisy.

"A what?"

"I gather up driftwood from the river and sell it for firewood at the market. And I dip for sardines too. Ain't nothin' else to do round here. All the work comes from the river."

"And your parents?"

"Never met 'em."

"Oh," said Bartholomew. "Well. And you live in a swamp."

"Yep."

Bartholomew cooked under the sun and looked at the passing scenery. Every once in a while they would pass a house, a grand old house with columns and huge trees out front. But all of these grand houses looked ruined somehow, graying and leaning. The strange moss hanging from the trees tried to protect the embarrassed faces of these proud houses, but stares from the road could still get through. Bartholomew was a thousand miles away from New York City but it felt even further.

"How far away are we from Ascension Parish?" asked Bartholomew.

"Dunno," said Daisy. "Probably get there tomorrow afternoon."

"Tomorrow afternoon!" cried Bartholomew. "But where shall we sleep, and what shall we do about eating?"

"Monk'll have somethin' cookin'," promised Daisy.

"*Monk?* As in Monk Swamp? It's named after a real person?"

But Daisy didn't answer him. The wagon rolled on, and eventually the sun started to sink behind the trees in the west and Daisy headed the wagon off the road. Soon they reached the shore of a big bog and Bartholomew saw a sign nailed to a tree that read:

Bayou Respond Pas
also known as
"Monk Swamp"
No Tresspassing

" 'Bayou Respond Pas,' " Bartholomew read aloud. "What does it mean?"

"It's French for 'no response swamp,' " said Daisy. " 'Cause there's no echo."

"What do you mean?"

"You can shout into any other swamp and you hear an echo, but not here. Try it."

"Oh, that's not necessary," said Bartholomew. "I believe you."

"Go on then," coaxed Daisy.

Feeling rather silly, Bartholomew shouted out the first word that came to mind:

"Tennyson!"

But Daisy was right and no echo came. The sound of his voice just blew like powder into the steam and mist.

"Told you," said Daisy. "They say there's a ghost in there who wants to talk again real bad. So he captures your echo and tries to use it. That's why you shouldn't shout too many times here, in case he gets your voice for good."

They rode along at the edge of the swamp until they arrived at a clearing with several rickety shanties. Dozens of fur hides hung from the walls.

"Those are Monk's," Daisy told Bartholomew. "He's a trapper. That's him over there."

Sure enough, an old man with a matted beard stood chopping onions over an iron pot on a campfire. He looked Bartholomew up and down and didn't utter a single word.

"You can sleep here tonight," said Daisy, hanging up the precious velvet cape on a nail next to a fetid raccoon hide. "And we'll start out again for Ascension Parish tomorrow mornin'."

"What's in that pot?" asked Bartholomew hungrily.

"Stew," said Monk. He doled out some of the stew onto a tin plate and handed it to Bartholomew, who wolfed it down.

"This is a delicious stew," he announced. "What's in it?"

"Neighbor's cat," croaked Monk, grinning toothlessly as Bartholomew spit it out onto the plate. Daisy thought this was a fine joke as well, and he and Monk laughed and chortled together.

"He's just foolin'," said Daisy. "But the rule round here is this: if it flies over the swamp, walks in the swamp, or swims in the swamp, it better watch out. 'Cause Monk here will catch and cook just 'bout anythin'."

For the first time in his life, Bartholomew put down a plate of food. He looked at it sitting there on the ground and thought of his Sardi's pork chops a world away and felt like crying.

"Aw, it's just possum," said Daisy, ladling some out for himself. "Set down and eat some supper. Say, what're you lookin' for down here anyway?"

"I may as well tell you," said Bartholomew. "You might be of some help to me. Do you know the name Fontaine?"

"You mean the Fontaines from Aigredoux?" asked Daisy.

"Yes, yes!" cried Bartholomew. "Do you mean to tell me that Aigredoux is a real place? How do you know them?"

"Everyone knows everyone else down here," said Daisy. "I mean, they wouldn't talk to no dirt like me, but I know about 'em."

"What can you tell me about them?"

"The Fontaines been there forever," said Daisy. "They used to be real rich, but now that house is comin' apart at the seams and most of 'em are gone. The only Fontaine left at Aigredoux is Miz Henrietta."

"Doesn't a gentleman named Tennyson Fontaine live there as well?" asked Bartholomew with great concern.

"I ain't heard of Tennyson Fontaine," said Daisy. "Miz Henrietta's married to ole Twigs Duvol. 'Course he's from an old family too. Used to be that Old Money married Old Money and made more money. These days, No More Old Money marries No More Old Money and they *still* act all high-'n'-mighty."

"Get back to the family, please," Bartholomew said snippily.

"Well, ole Twigs fell off his horse a long time ago and has been actin' sorta strange ever since," said Daisy. "So Miz Henrietta's runnin' the house. There's supposed to be sort of an old curse on the Fontaine women, that the men in the family all die off or go crazy or leave 'em at Aigredoux alone."

"We must leave for Aigredoux first thing in the morning!" implored Bartholomew. "It must be the right place, I'm sure of it!"

"All right," said Daisy. "If the house is still standin'."

It was dark by then and the swamp was filled with strange noises, including the rumbling of Bartholomew's stomach. Old Monk sat by the fire, and when he finished eating his share of possum stew, he sang them a raucous song and clapped in time:

> *Juba, Juba,*
> *Juba up 'n' Juba down,*
> *Juba all over the town.*
> *Juba, Juba,*
> *Juba this 'n' Juba that,*
> *Juba killed the yaller cat.*
> *Juba, Juba,*
> *Juba left 'n' Juba right,*
> *Juba, Juba, gettin' night.*

This song made no sense to Bartholomew but Daisy clapped along and seemed to enjoy it a great deal. Then Monk offered

Bartholomew some whisky, so he took it and drank it and soon he fell asleep right there in the dirt next to the campfire. He snored so loudly that no one had to worry about any creatures or the voice-stealing ghost coming out of the swamp to surprise them.

When Bartholomew woke up in the middle of the night, he found that Daisy had thoughtfully covered him with the red-velvet-lined cape. This kind gesture almost made tears smart Bartholomew's eyes, and for a moment he almost forgot that he, the great Bartholomew Prentiss of the *Sophisticate,* had been robbed and forced to travel with chickens and sardines, and was currently residing in a swamp with a toothless trapper named Monk who liked to cook cats.

He nestled down under his cape and fell back asleep.

Chapter Sixteen

WHITEWASH

Aunt Henrietta hadn't been feeling very well since her letter came from Washington, D.C. And so when she came downstairs for the first time in nearly a week to write a letter in the ladies' parlor, everyone was surprised.

"Does Aunt Henrietta need me to go to the post office for her?" Tennyson asked Zulma.

Zulma turned to Hattie and said, "Tell your sister that she ain't takin' the mail out anymore. I'm gonna do it."

"Why don't you tell her?" asked Hattie. "She's standing right here."

"Don't sass me," said Zulma, and walked out of the house with the letter.

And then, everyone got surprised again the next day when

someone knocked at the front door. Tennyson answered it. A servant who wore clothes like Zulma stood on the porch.

"I'm Rosalie, from Belmont," said the woman.

Tennyson looked at her blankly.

"You know, *Belmont*," she said. "Big house up the river road. I've got a reply letter here for Miz Henrietta."

When Rosalie left and Tennyson gave Aunt Henrietta the letter, she disappeared with it into her parlor. After a minute, she came out again and her face was filled with anxious hope. She and Zulma bent their heads together and whispered.

"Come on, we've got a whole lotta work to do," Zulma told Hattie. "Bring your sister," she added, even though Tennyson was of course standing right there. And they all went out into the backyard. Zulma pulled a huge metal basin out of one of the broken shacks.

"Help me lug this sack over to the basin," she hollered to Hattie, tugging a heavy burlap bag out of the shack. "Don't get any on your hands."

"What is it?" Hattie asked.

"Lime."

"What for?"

"We're makin' whitewash."

Zulma poured the lime into the basin and added salt and water and stirred, and soon a white liquid appeared.

"What's this for?" asked Hattie, covering her nose with the hem of her dress.

"We're gonna whitewash all the downstairs floors in

the house," Zulma said. "They used to use this on slave cabins 'stead of paint, but it's the best we've got. Aigredoux's gotta sparkle from top to bottom. We've got a visitor comin' tomorrow."

"Who?" cried Hattie. "Is Papa coming back? Did he find Mama?"

"No, he's not, and no, he didn't," said Zulma. "Grab the edge of the basin and quit squawkin'."

They dragged the tub into the house. Then they opened every door and window to let the fumes out and slopped the whitewash over the splintery wood floors. It took many hours because Aigredoux was so big and the floors drank up all the whitewash so thirstily. When they were done, Zulma washed her hands with vinegar and the girls did the same.

"I'm so tired," said Hattie, sitting down on the floor.

"Get up off that floor," cried Zulma. "Look at your backside." The seat of the dress was stained white from the wash.

A hammer pounded outside on the front porch.

"Mister Thomas is tryin' to rebuild the front stairs," Zulma explained.

They filed out onto the porch to see how Uncle Twigs was making out. He squinted up at them from under a tattered panama hat.

"This is *quite* a bit more difficult than it looks," he said. The stairs looked just awful, crooked and wobbly. Hattie giggled.

Aunt Henrietta swept out of the front yard, her arms filled with weedy field flowers.

"These must fill every room," she said. "I want Aigredoux to remind our visitor of Persephone in springtime."

"What's Persephone, and *who is the visitor*?" asked Hattie as Aunt Henrietta shoved flowers into her arms, but no one bothered to answer her, as usual.

Everyone brought flowers inside, and when they ran out of vases, they stuffed the flowers into buckets and pots and put them in all of the downstairs rooms. It was dark outside by then and Hattie and Tennyson were hungry and exhausted.

"Go help yourself to some grits and biscuits," Zulma said. "And after that, come straight back. We've still got more to do."

The girls trudged off to the kitchen.

"I'm so tired I can't even lift my spoon," complained Hattie. "What's going on? Why won't they tell us who's coming?"

Tennyson shrugged, rubbing her own aching arms. "I don't know."

"And why's Zulma acting like that? Why won't she talk to you?"

Tennyson hesitated. Zulma hadn't spoken to Tennyson directly since the night she'd found and burned Tennyson's stories. The whole trauma of being discovered and having her plans thwarted had left Tennyson broken and numb and she did not feel like explaining it all to Hattie.

"I guess she's mad at me about something," she said cautiously. "Who knows."

"Everyone's always mad about *something* around here," said Hattie crossly. "I want to go to bed."

But the hardest work of all was waiting for them when they finished their dinner, work that made Hattie cry and even made Tennyson lose her temper. They had to help Zulma and Aunt Henrietta and Uncle Twigs rip the vines off the front of the house. The vines were in a worse mood than ever and refused to come down, and some of them were so thick that Uncle Twigs had to cut them up with a handsaw. Soon everyone was covered in plaster dust from the front of the house, and they stopped pulling only when the brick underneath the plaster started to show through.

"That's enough," declared Aunt Henrietta. "You girls go up to bed. You both must look fresh as flowers tomorrow."

"Wait a minute." Zulma followed the girls into the weed-flower-filled Hall of Ancestors. "Hand over those clothes."

Plaster crumbled from the dresses onto the whitewashed floors.

"Give yourselves a good scrubbin' before you get into that bed," Zulma admonished, marching with the dresses toward the kitchen. But Hattie and Tennyson ignored the wash bucket in their room and fell straight into bed.

And God only knows if Zulma went to sleep at all. When Hattie and Tennyson woke up the next morning, their dresses had been washed and mended and even had new sashes sewn onto them, and Zulma was out whitewashing the front porch.

The visitor was coming.

***

The girls went into the kitchen to help themselves to some breakfast grits, but no pots gurgled on the stove.

Zulma came in, looking surly and tired. "Go meet Miz Henrietta in the ladies' parlor," she told them.

"Isn't there anything to eat?" asked Hattie.

"Your aunt said no breakfast today," Zulma said. "She said that you have to look slim for your visitor. Now get goin'."

The parlor was empty, and the girls sat on their hard bench.

"Good morning," sang out Aunt Henrietta as she sailed into the room and closed the door behind her.

Tennyson and Hattie stared at their aunt, who had undergone the most astonishing transformation overnight. Her hair hung in ringlets around her face and ribbons adorned her wrists and neck. Smears of pink rouge tinged her cheeks and lips, and her dress had also been washed and sported a new sash.

"Zulma has done wonders with your garments," Aunt Henrietta observed. "Try not to ruin them," she added, looking darkly at Tennyson. She put down a basket filled with rag strips and pulled out a comb.

"Let's get to work," she said, dragging the comb through Hattie's tangled hair.

"Owww!" screamed Hattie, covering her head with her arms. "What are you doing?"

"These are rag curlers," said Aunt Henrietta impatiently. "We can't have you looking like this when the visitor arrives, can we? Now hold still." She tried to pull the comb through Hattie's snarls again, producing another series of shrieks. Bondurant waddled up to the window to watch and added a nasty little scream of his own.

"I don't *want* rag curls!" Hattie yelled, leaping up off the bench and taking refuge behind Louvenia's dusty harp.

"You're getting your dress dirty!" cried Aunt Henrietta. "Come out from behind there this instant."

"Not until you tell us what's going on," shouted Hattie. The harp lurched and tinkled violently.

"Fine." Aunt Henrietta gave in. "Come over here and behave yourself."

Hattie came out from behind the harp and sat down next to Tennyson. Aunt Henrietta sat in a chair in front of them. The three of them stared at each other silently.

Aunt Henrietta pursed her lips. "Ladies," she said at last. "Today is a very important day, one that you will remember forever. For on this day, you will receive your first suitor."

"What?" cried Hattie.

"Your first gentleman caller," said Aunt Henrietta. Tennyson sat up in alarm.

"Ewww," shouted Hattie. "Who?"

"None other than young Mr. Perrault Bossier of Belmont," Aunt Henrietta informed them.

"That's the stupidest name I've ever heard," said Hattie, resuming her station behind the harp.

"Aunt Henrietta, Hattie's only eight," Tennyson protested. "And I'm only eleven. We're too young for a suitor."

"I *know* that," fussed Aunt Henrietta defensively. "But there's no harm in getting acquainted, is there? If nothing else, it will be nice to renew the Fontaine friendship with the Bossiers. They were smart. They put their money in New York banks during the war and they're still rich. Mr. Perrault is coming at five for an early supper."

She left the room and came back with a tall candle, which she wedged into the special courtship candleholder.

"I'm going to help Zulma in the kitchen," she said. "Roll your hair up in those rags so it gets nice and curly. And rub some of this on your wrists and sprinkle it in your hair so you smell nice." She left a little jar of nutmeg on a table by the door and swished girlishly out of the room again.

Tennyson and Hattie stared at each other in dismay.

"She's completely lost her mind," said Hattie. "They've *all* gone crazy. Let's run away."

"But what if we run away and Papa comes back?" Tennyson asked. "He won't know where we are."

"I don't want to wear rag curlers," whimpered Hattie. "Or meet that stupid boy. What are we going to do?"

"I don't think there's anything that we *can* do," said Tennyson. "We just need something to happen."

Indeed, Tennyson and Hattie very much needed something to happen. Tennyson had already tried to make something happen on her own, and she had learned the hard way that that's not how things worked around here. Around here, you just had to pray for the utterly unlikely to come true. You had to pray that your father would somehow find your mother, who clearly didn't want to be found. You had to pray that the Mississippi wouldn't decide one day to come out of its bed behind the levee and swallow up the house. You had to pray that a spoiled boy named Perrault Bossier would take a liking to one of your nieces and that somehow his family's money would seep into Aigredoux's foundations and steel it up.

But then something *did* happen.

It started to rain. First several fat drops splattered on the windows and a sullen rumble of thunder came from the river. Then came more fat drops, and more, and the sky turned purple.

Aunt Henrietta and Zulma came out of the kitchen and fretfully watched the storm from the front door.

"Don't worry, it's just a cloudburst," Zulma said. "It'll pass."

But it didn't pass. It rained harder and harder, and soon all of the whitewash on the front porch and the crooked new steps drained away and formed ugly, chalky puddles in the front yard.

"Let's just keep cookin'," said Zulma when tears threatened to interfere with Aunt Henrietta's rouge. "He'll be here." They disappeared back into the kitchen.

Hattie grew more and more gleeful as the sky grew darker.

"Ha," she said, kicking the basket of rag curlers to the floor. "Take that."

"Pick those up before Aunt Henrietta sees them," said Tennyson, starting to feel slightly guilty, as though she'd conjured up this storm herself. The yard was turning to mud under the vines and the ghost moss in the trees sagged and dripped.

Soon delicious smells wafted up from the kitchen and Zulma called the girls out of the parlor to help set the very long dining room table.

"Mr. Bossier is gonna sit next to Mr. Thomas," she instructed. "And don't forget to set the empty place on the other side."

A terrific crack of thunder shook the house. Tennyson glanced up at the portraits of Atlas and Julia and thought that even they looked anxious.

"What're we eating for dinner?" asked Hattie, clattering a plate onto the table.

"It's gonna be a feast," said Zulma. "You're startin' with turtle 'n' sherry soup and then havin' pheasant. After that, you're movin' on to a fine Virginia ham."

Tennyson wondered how much of the marble stairs money went to buying that meal for the Bossier boy and if any of that money was left. But everyone was already on edge so she decided not to ask.

Soon the table was set and the beautiful meal was almost ready, and still it rained. Aunt Henrietta paced in the front hallway and fidgeted with her ribbons.

"What time is it?" she asked Uncle Twigs. He was sitting at his desk in the gentlemen's parlor, writing letters. All week he had been writing letters, angry letters of protest to the other members of the Louisiana Society for the Strict Enforcement of the Proper Use of the English Language.

"It is nearly five o'clock now," he answered, consulting an ancient rusted pocket watch.

"Oh, he's not going to come," wailed Aunt Henrietta. "I just know it. All of this has been for nothing. We're *ruined*."

"Now don't get carried away, Miz Henrietta," said Zulma. "It ain't even time for him to be here yet."

But then Uncle Twigs's pocket watch read five o'clock, and then five-fifteen, and then five-thirty. Tears rolled down Aunt Henrietta's face, and even Hattie started to feel bad.

"He's probably just stuck in the mud, that's all," said Zulma. "Why don't you and Mister Thomas and the girls go into the dining room, and I'll give you that fine soup."

"Thank you, Zulma," said Aunt Henrietta, dabbing at her face with a lace hanky. "You've been very kind."

The family settled down at their place settings and Zulma brought in the turtle and sherry soup.

"At last," said Uncle Twigs, his monocle happily glinting in the candlelight.

Just then, someone knocked on the front door.

Aunt Henrietta shot up out of her seat. "Lord in heaven," she cried. "He came. Through all of this mud and rain and wind," and tears welled in her eyes again. "Thomas—go answer the door."

Uncle Twigs bumbled out of the dining room.

"Girls, stand up straight," hissed Aunt Henrietta. "Look

appealing." And she smiled sweetly and stared at the dining room door, willing Mr. Perrault Bossier to make his entrance.

Uncle Twigs's footsteps thumped up to the front door and then came the sound of the latch lifting.

"Good evening," said Uncle Twigs's voice. "Oh, my. You're *quite* a bit larger than I expected. But do come in, Mr. Bossier."

Aunt Henrietta beamed.

"Bossier?" said a deep voice. "I am not Mr. Bossier."

"Why, then who are you?"

"Allow me to introduce myself," said the voice. "My name is Bartholomew Prentiss."

Chapter Seventeen

SELFISH

A confused silence reigned in the hallway. Tennyson's heart and head pounded in disbelief.

"Are—are we acquainted?" asked Uncle Twigs.

"Not exactly," said Bartholomew. "I am looking for a Mr. Tennyson Fontaine, who I assume is a relation of yours."

Zulma sucked in her breath and glared at Tennyson, and Hattie looked at her sister with wide eyes. Tennyson wanted to crawl under the table, but shock spiked into her limbs and froze them.

"*Mister* Tennyson Fontaine?" cried Aunt Henrietta. "What's going on?"

A drenched Bartholomew charged into the room. "You must be Henrietta!" he said.

Aunt Henrietta gasped. Under other circumstances, Bartholomew Prentiss of the *Sophisticate* might have been considered a somewhat respectable caller (even though he was a certified Yankee), due to his dandy three-piece suit and lofty manners and Fontaine-like sense of superiority. Uncle Twigs might have admired Bartholomew's impressive vocabulary and floral use of words. The men might have retired to the gentlemen's parlor after dinner with the leftover sherry from the turtle and sherry soup and discussed the significance of gerunds and their mutual hatred for dangling participles.

But not on this evening.

Certainly not on this evening, for mud and dirt and chicken feathers adorned the soggy three-piece suit. The faint smell of sardines wafted through the room along with the suit's wearer, and little puddles eked out of his shoes at every step.

"Yes, I am Henrietta Fontaine-Duvol." Aunt Henrietta drew herself up to her full terrible height. "But who are you?"

"I am Bartholomew Prentiss, the editor of the *Sophisticate* magazine," Bartholomew announced, and paused dramatically, waiting for the awe to sink in. "As I'm sure you are aware, I have published the first two chapters of Mr. Tennyson Fontaine's book about the tormented saga of Aigredoux and the Fontaine family. I have traveled over a thousand miles to offer him a contract to complete the book for the magazine. The world hungrily awaits the remainder of his masterpiece."

Aunt Henrietta's poor mind was clearly staggering about inside her head.

"He's crazy, Zulma," she said, gripping the side of the table. "On top of *everything* else, we now have a crazy hobo in our dining room. Quick—grab the fireplace poker. We have to get him out of here."

"Did you say the *Sophisticate* magazine?" asked Uncle Twigs, narrowing his eyes. "*Quite* a blasphemous publication—run by anarchists, rabble-rousers, and communists!"

"I *beg* your pardon!" said Bartholomew. "It most certainly is not! And how dare you question my sanity, you impudent woman! Don't you know who I *am*? Where is Mr. Tennyson? I demand an audience with him at once."

Zulma marched across the room and grabbed Tennyson by her ear.

"*This* is Mr. Tennyson Fontaine," she said. "Bet you feel the fool now, don't you?"

"I am not in the mood for practical jokes, madam," cried Bartholomew. "If only you knew what I've been through to get here, and now, to be received in such a manner!" To his humiliation, a little tear rolled down the side of his dirty nose.

Tennyson wrenched herself away from Zulma.

"It's true," she said to Bartholomew. "I wrote those stories."

"Oh, hush up," said Bartholomew, wiping away his tear. "I'm in no mood to deal with brats."

"It really was me," Tennyson said, and something in her old-child demeanor suddenly told Bartholomew that she was telling the truth. "I wrote both of those chapters. 'The Tragedy of

Louvenia Fontaine' and 'Before the Storm.' How would I know what they were called if I didn't write them?"

Aunt Henrietta reached her boiling point and her horrified wrath spilled over.

"How could you!" she screamed, and threw a soup spoon at Tennyson. "After everything we've done for you—fed you, clothed you, catered to your every need. We are your *family*. How could you betray us?"

Then she flung a teaspoon, but when she reached for a fork, Zulma rushed over to calm her.

"It's all right, Miz Henrietta," she said, taking Aunt Henrietta's hands. "I stopped her from writin' and sendin' those stories off. You don't have to worry 'bout it ever again."

"You *knew* about this?" cried Aunt Henrietta, pushing Zulma away. She tore up a handful of weed flowers from the centerpiece and flung them in Tennyson's direction. "What horrible lies have you been telling about our family?"

"Everything that I wrote was true," shouted Tennyson. Even her own voice was shocked to be shouting for once and everyone stared at her. "You're the one who lies about Aigredoux. The whole way you see it is a lie. You never see all the bad things that happened here, and when you do, you cover them up—it's all whitewash. All you care about is the sold marble and the stolen jewels and you just feel sorry for yourself that you weren't born in the old days so you could play God too—and live in a temple that your family built to worship itself."

Aunt Henrietta swayed slightly and touched her throat with her fingertips. Suddenly she was a dead woman, her eyes glassy and her skin waxy and white under the sad rouge. When she spoke, her voice was flat:

"Go away. Just *go away.*"

Tennyson ran out of the dining room and Hattie followed her.

Bartholomew sat down and stared at the table, stupefied. It was all too much. His beloved protégé, the author of the next great American novel, was a *child*—and on top of that, a *girl*. The thundercloud Mr. Nusselbaum appeared in his mind again, lightning bolts and all.

"That's it for you, Big Boy," shouted the cloud. "You're finished, through, done!"

Shut up, Bartholomew told the cloud viciously inside his mind. *I'll deal with you later.*

Aunt Henrietta sank into her chair and covered her face with her hands. After a minute, she placed her palms on the table and said to Bartholomew:

"Mr. Prentiss. I am very sorry if our niece has inconvenienced you in any way. And I am also sorry that you have made this very long journey for nothing. As long as that horrible child lives in my house, she will write no more stories about the Fontaines or Aigredoux. We have our reputation and our position in society to consider."

A chunk of wet plaster fell from the ceiling.

Bartholomew waded slowly out of his shock.

"I suspect, madam, that you are making a grave mistake," he began, in an effort to salvage Art. "Her fame is already—"

"We are one of the oldest families in Louisiana," said Aunt Henrietta. "We are not concerned with the sort of fame you are offering. I will not permit any further publications, and nor will I, as her guardian, sign any contracts on her behalf. You are at a dead end. Please see yourself out."

Rain beat against the windows.

"But I have nowhere to go," pleaded Bartholomew. "My ride will be halfway back to Monk Swamp by now."

Aunt Henrietta closed her eyes again and shook her head.

"Fine," she said, weary now. "I am bound by the code of Southern hospitality to offer you a room for the night, but please leave first thing in the morning. And make your presence as little felt as possible."

And with that she reached over and snuffed out the candles with her bare fingers. Then she left the room.

"Anarchists and communists," Uncle Twigs muttered, looking at Bartholomew darkly as he followed his wife out of the dining room.

Bartholomew sagged in his chair and looked up at Zulma.

"I'm afraid," he said, "that Fate has not been kind to me today."

"Welcome to Aigredoux," she said. "S'pose you've guessed by now that the Fontaines and Fate ain't on real good terms. Want some ham?"

This took Bartholomew by surprise.

"Well," he said. "It *would* be a shame to let it go to waste, now, wouldn't it?"

❖❖❖

That night Aigredoux made noises as it soaked up the rain. It sounded to Tennyson and Hattie like the house was moaning and saying very sad things in its own language. They lay under their bed because the mosquito net above their bed was sagging under the weight of fallen damp ceiling plaster.

Hattie was completely distraught from the scene downstairs so Tennyson left the oil lamp burning to comfort her. It was the middle of the night before Hattie fell asleep, breathing through her mouth as usual.

Tennyson pressed her cheek and ear to the floorboards and tried to understand what the house was saying. She felt bad about the terrible things she'd said to Aunt Henrietta, even though they had all been true. But it was funny: Tennyson knew that Aigredoux was built on misery and pain, but despite this, she found that she loved the house now too, and she felt that it loved her back.

That's what the Mississippi does. It tempts you in, and then it catches you. It loves you and doesn't want to let you go. So it pulls you down to the bottom and keeps you there.

Maybe that's why Emery knew the Mississippi so well. Because he'd had so much practice getting tempted and caught by Aigredoux, which pulled as fiercely as any river current.

Footsteps padded up to the door, and then came a quiet knock.

"Who is it," whispered Tennyson into the upside-down keyhole.

A whisper came back: "It's Bartholomew Prentiss. I have something for you."

Tennyson opened the door. Bartholomew was holding an alligator suitcase that had been puckered and ruined by the rain.

"It is still dry on the inside," he said when he was inside the room and the door was closed. "That suitcase is of the finest quality, I assure you."

"What's inside?"

"Look for yourself."

Tennyson took the case. "I still can't believe that you're here," she told him.

"I still cannot believe that you're a child," said Bartholomew, unable to conceal his dismay.

"Well, I can't believe that you published my stories."

"And I cannot believe that you won't be able to finish your book about Aigredoux," said Bartholomew sadly. And then, with more determination: "I refuse to accept it. That beastly Henrietta cannot prevent Art."

"Yes," said Tennyson. "I'm afraid she can."

"She's appallingly selfish," Bartholomew growled. "You could be an important writer."

"That's not why I sent you the stories. And anyway, I can't be an important writer."

"What? Why not?"

"I'm not allowed," Tennyson said.

Bartholomew stood up very straight. "We'll find a way around that gorgon of an aunt, I promise."

"But she's not the real reason I can't become a writer."

"Then who is preventing you?"

Tennyson stared at the lamp. "Can I ask you a question, Mr. Prentiss?" she asked after a minute.

"I suppose so," said Bartholomew, who was very overwrought and confused by now.

"Do you remember reading any stories and poems from a woman named Sadie?" asked Tennyson.

"Who is she?"

"Someone I know, someone who sends you stories all the time."

"Nothing comes to mind," said Bartholomew. "I remember what is truly fine, and the rest I throw away and forget. Clearly this Sadie character is a mediocre talent, while you are not." He did not understand why this proclamation made Tennyson look sad when it should have made her proud.

"Open the suitcase," he urged. "Its contents will prove my point exactly."

Dozens of letters fell out of their warped alligator cocoon.

"What are all these letters?"

"Fan letters," said Bartholomew regally. "Why don't you

peruse some of them while I come up with some sort of masterful plan for you to finish your book right away." He wished that he had his special red-velvet-lined cape. He always came up with clever plans when he wore it.

While Bartholomew scowled and sighed and thought, Tennyson opened a few of the letters. The praise in them embarrassed her and even made her a little ashamed of herself, because she had not written her stories for these people who loved them.

And then she saw it.

The handwriting on the envelope was slightly different than usual, but that's because the writer didn't have her special pen, the pen she always used.

Tennyson had it.

She opened the letter.

My dear Tennyson,

I do not know exactly where you are right now—have you been at Aigredoux of all places? Are you still there? I don't dare send you a note there, since I know that Henrietta would happily burn it up and make sure that you never saw it. So this seems the best way, to send it to the magazine.

In any case, I can hardly believe that your father would have left you there, considering how he hates it so much and that his whole life he has railed against it. All I do know for sure is that you and your sister are not at home, at Innisfree. I know this because I know your father and his endless love for me, and I'm sure that he is out looking for me.

I have seen your beautiful stories in the Sophisticate, *and when I got over the shock of seeing your name there, I was filled with pride—and of course jealousy. To think that you have achieved my life goal at the tender age of eleven and captured the imagination of thousands of readers! You are a true marvel and a beautiful writer. I can hardly believe that I created you.*

And because I know you as I know your father, I sensed something about these stories . . . were they written for me? I think that they were. And I just want you to know that I understood this, and I think that I understood what you were saying to me in those stories. My poor Tennyson, you have always worked so hard to keep me from leaving; you've worked so hard to make me understand the beauty in our own family. And I always fought against you and refused to see.

You were right of course; your stories prove it. I believe that you were urging me to come home, telling me that there was still inspiration to be found there, even if it's based on realities that we'd rather not face. Fontaines are never very good about facing realities, are they? Except for you, wise owl.

I am a failure, Tennyson. I am a failure as a wife and a mother, and now I am a failure as a writer. I could not even see poetry that was so plain to an eleven-year-old girl. There is no way to soften the blow of what I am going to say next. I am not coming home. Please try to understand. No matter how much you hate me at first, you can be sure that I hate myself even more. Please don't see this as a failure on your part. I love you for what you tried to do and how you did it, and it will be our special secret forever. I am selfish, Tennyson, and a coward. But I love you no matter what. Maybe when you're older, you will understand and even forgive me.

Don't worry, your father will come and get you soon and take you back to Innisfree. Because when he can't find me, he'll remember that the only part of me that he has left is in his daughters.

I hope that the people at the magazine send this note

*to you, wherever you are. Take good care of your sister and
father, and say hello to Jos next time he comes around
for supper.*

All my love and blessings,
Mama

♦♦♦

As you know by now, Tennyson rarely cried. Everyone else
around her cried. Hattie. Aunt Henrietta. The faithless Sadie
and even the faithful Emery. Tennyson was exhausted from all
of the tears. And anyway, tears wouldn't change Sadie's mind,
Tennyson told herself, and they wouldn't keep Aigredoux from
rotting. Tears wouldn't change anything.

But they came anyway, so many of them that Tennyson
couldn't even breathe.

Suddenly everything was decided and nothing was solved.

And then, in that terrible vague space between success and
failure, Tennyson was no longer an old child. She felt like a
grown-up, just like that. Like Sadie herself had probably felt
when baby Tennyson had first come into her world. Tennyson
didn't know what it all meant, if it was supposed to mean something bigger, if it was supposed to turn out like this all along. All
she knew was that she just wanted to keep crying until her eyelids closed and sleep came, a dreamless sleep.

"Good heavens, what's the matter?" exclaimed Bartholomew when he saw what was happening.

Tennyson pulled her knees into her chest and rocked back

and forth. The tears wouldn't let her talk for a long time, and when they did, she said:

"Now it's *really* over."

"What's over?" cried Bartholomew in alarm, and when Tennyson put her forehead on her knees and didn't answer him, he took Sadie's letter and read it.

For the first time in his life, Bartholomew Prentiss was at a loss for words.

And so this man, usually awkward as a turnip, did what any warm-blooded human being would do. He reached out and held Tennyson's hand. Because there was nothing else he could do, nothing else in the world he or anyone could give her.

Tennyson accepted the comfort of this stranger. She accepted the comfort of Bartholomew's soft hand and the comfort of the house, which wrapped her in its heartbeat and slowly lulled her to sleep.

Chapter Eighteen

RELEASE

A few years earlier, Emery had come home to Innisfree carrying a stack of heavy old books.

"These are for you," he told Tennyson and Hattie.

"What are they—stories?" asked Hattie.

"Yes, the best sort," said Emery. "Because they're real stories. These are history books."

Each evening he would read out loud from those books, and this counted as school. That's how Caesar and Napoleon and Abraham Lincoln came to the rickety house on stilts in the middle of nowhere.

Hattie grew restless during one of the lessons.

"I'm tired of these real stories," she said. "I want a fake one, like we used to read. I want *Alice in Wonderland*."

"It's important that you learn about history," Emery said, looking up from his reading.

"Why?"

"Because people who don't know history are bound to repeat it," he said. "We have to learn from other people's successes and failures."

Tennyson had not been restless during the history lessons. She had listened very closely.

"I think people are bound to repeat history no matter what," she said.

"What do you mean?" Emery asked.

"All we've heard about are big wars," Tennyson said. "Since the beginning of time. Everyone reads about how horrible wars are, but there are always new wars. So it doesn't seem like there's a choice; people never learn and just repeat history all the time."

"Now listen to me very closely," Emery said. "Everyone has a choice to break with the past or get caught up in it. Always. It's one of the most important lessons I can ever teach you."

He closed his book.

That had been a lovely night. Sadie had finished writing a good poem, and this had made her happy. She even cooked a special dinner, a gumbo. Then Jos came by to visit, and everyone laughed because he had a red silk ribbon tied around his neck. The family teased him about his mystery double life and called him a dandy.

They didn't know it, but that night they were living inside

Emery's warm dream, one that he'd made come true by knowing the past and not making other people's mistakes.

And knowing that he had the choice.

✦✦✦

Tennyson had a choice now too.

"I have to leave," said a voice, and she opened her eyes. The room was filled with gray dawn light.

Bartholomew looked down at her sadly.

"I'm very sorry about your mother," he said.

Tennyson nodded.

"But don't worry," Bartholomew assured her. "We will find a way for you to finish your beautiful book."

"I'm not writing any more of the book," whispered Tennyson, careful not to wake Hattie. "There's no point. Especially now."

"Of *course* there's a point," said Bartholomew. "You cannot give up."

"I have work to do," Tennyson told him.

"What work?"

"I have to take care of my family."

"But writing is your calling," Bartholomew pressed, almost desperately. "Surely nothing can be more important than—"

They both looked down at Sadie's letter, lying there on the floor.

It was quiet then. There was only the fluttering of birds' wings in the tree outside the window.

Suddenly Bartholomew thought about Mr. Nusselbaum and Pink Duveen and Hollywood and how they'd sent him down here, scurrying after a prize they wanted for all the wrong reasons. And then he realized that for the first time in years, he had a *real* chance to be a Servant of Art. Not by trying to rope Tennyson in, but by letting her go. By protecting her and Aigredoux and the rest of the sad story that went along with them until that story was ready to be told.

"To Hades with all of you!" he told his boss and Miss Duveen and even the *Sophisticate* in his mind, and then he felt light as a feather. He hadn't felt this sharp sort of happiness since he'd discovered his red-velvet-lined cape, hanging up in a store window.

"Promise me something," he said to Tennyson, his big hands trembling. "Just one thing."

"What?"

"That you will write the rest of the book and send it to me, when you're older and on your own."

"Send it to you at the magazine?"

"As of this moment, I am no longer affiliated with the *Sophisticate* magazine," Bartholomew said, and to his surprise he felt almost giddy. "But wherever I am, I'll make sure that your beautiful book gets into the right hands and keep it out of the wrong ones."

Tennyson watched him, wondering why his face suddenly looked so bright.

"What do you say?" Bartholomew asked.

Tennyson stared at her hands and thought.

Sadie was gone. The barbed fence around Sadie's dream was gone too. Maybe that dream could belong to Tennyson now, the one about being a great writer. Maybe it was time for Tennyson to have her own dream at last.

Everyone has a choice.

Always.

Tennyson looked up at Bartholomew.

"All right," she told him. "I promise."

Sometimes the Mississippi lets the little girls at the bottom go after all.

The End

Appendix

Fontaine Family Tree

Atlas Fontaine — Julia Bessinon
(1808 - 1866)   (1811 - 1878)

Pierre Fontaine   John Fontaine   Jouvenix Fontaine   Langdon Fontaine   Henry Fontaine
(1840 - 1841)   (1842 - 1862)   (1838 - 1888)   (1837 - 1863)   (1848 - ?)

Thomas Fontaine — Hattie Lee Middleton
(1843 - 1882)   (1848 - 1868)

Pemberton Fontaine — Jay Allston
(1868 - 1915)   (1871 - 1920)

Barnwell Fontaine   Henriette Fontaine — Thomas Duval
(1893 - 1916)   (1895 - 1944)   (1890 - 1954)

Sadie Ventress — Emory Fontaine
(1901 - ?)   (1898 - 1963)

Tennyson Fontaine (1921 -)   Hattie Fontaine
                                     (1924 -)

Fontaine Family History, from Bible of Henriette Fontaine

1808 - Atlas Fontaine born, Virginia

1811 - Julia Bessiner born, New Orleans

1829 - Atlas Fontaine weds Julia Bessiner, Aigredoux, LA

1837 - Langdon Fontaine born, Aigredoux, LA

1838 - Jouvencia Fontaine born, Aigredoux, LA

1840 - Pierre Fontaine born, Aigredoux, LA

1841 - Pierre Fontaine dies, fever, buried at Aigredoux

1842 - John Fontaine born, Aigredoux

1843 - Thomas Fontaine born, Aigredoux

1848 - Henry Fontaine born, Aigredoux

1862 - John Fontaine dies, battle at Second Manassas, buried on site

1863 - Langdon Fontaine dies, battle at Gettysburg, buried on site

1863 - Henry Fontaine disappears, taken POW)

1866 - Atlas Fontaine dies, suicide, buried at Aigredoux

1868 - Thomas Fontaine weds Hettie Lee Middleton, Aigredoux

1868 - Hettie Lee Middleton dies, childbirth, buried at Aigredoux

1868 - Pemberton Fontaine born, Aigredoux

1878 - Julia Bissiore Fontaine dies, natural causes, buried at Aigredoux

1882 - Thomas Fontaine dies, fever, buried at Aigredoux

1888 - Jouvena Fontaine dies in sleep, cause unclear, buried at Aigredoux

1891 - Pemberton Fontaine weds Lacy Allston, Aigredoux

1893 - Barnwell Fontaine born, Aigredoux

1895 - Henrietta Fontaine born, Aigredoux

1898 - Emery Fontaine born, Aigredoux

1913 - Henrietta Fontaine weds Thomas Duval

1915 - Pemberton Fontaine dies, horse accident, buried at Aigredoux

1916 - Barnwell Fontaine dies, battles France, First World War, buried on site

1920 - Lacy Allston Fontaine dies, suicide, buried in New Orleans

1920 - Emery Fontaine weds Sadie Ventress, New Orleans

1921 - Tennyson Fontaine born, Innisfree, MS

1924 - Hattie Fontaine born, Innisfree, MS

POEMS AND SONGS IN
TENNYSON

"The Lake Isle of Innisfree"

This is the poem that inspired the name of the Mississippi woods house of Emery, Sadie, Tennyson, and Hattie Fontaine.

I will arise and go now, and go to Innisfree,
And a small cabin build there, of clay and wattles made:
Nine bean-rows will I have there, a hive for the honeybee,
And live alone in the bee-loud glade.

And I shall have some peace there, for peace comes
   dropping slow,
Dropping from the veils of the morning to where the
   cricket sings;
There midnight's all a-glimmer, and noon a purple glow,
And evening full of the linnet's wings.

I will arise and go now, for always night and day
I hear lake water lapping with low sounds by the shore;
While I stand on the roadway, or on the pavements grey,
I hear it in the deep heart's core.

—William Butler Yeats

"The Deserted House"

This is another poem by Tennyson's namesake, poet Alfred, Lord Tennyson. It was Sadie's favorite poem and eerily reflects the state of Aigredoux by the time Tennyson and Hattie are staying there.

I.

Life and Thought have gone away
Side by side,
Leaving door and windows wide;
Careless tenants they!

II.

All within is dark as night:
In the windows is no light;
And no murmur at the door,
So frequent on its hinge before.

III.

Close the door, the shutters close,
Or thro' the windows we shall see
The nakedness and vacancy
Of the dark deserted house.

IV.

Come away; no more of mirth
Is here or merry-making sound.
The house was builded of the earth,
And shall fall again to ground.

V.

Come away; for Life and Thought
Here no longer dwell,
But in a city glorious—
A great and distant city—have bought
A mansion incorruptible.
Would they could have stayed with us!

"Nothing Will Die"

This is the Alfred, Lord Tennyson poem that Zipporah quotes to Tennyson.

When will the stream be aweary of flowing under my eye?
When will the wind be aweary of blowing over the sky?
When will the clouds be aweary of fleeting?
When will the heart be aweary of beating?
And nature die?
Never, O, never, nothing will die;
The stream flows,
The wind blows,
The cloud fleets,
The heart beats,
      Nothing will die.

Nothing will die;
All things will change
Thro' eternity.
'Tis the world's winter;
Autumn and summer
Are gone long ago;
Earth is dry to the centre,
But spring, a new comer,
A spring rich and strange,

Shall make the winds blow
Round and round,
Thro' and thro',
    Here and there,
    Till the air
And the ground
Shall be fill'd with life anew.

The world was never made;
It will change, but it will not fade.
So let the wind range;
For even and morn
    Ever will be
    Thro' eternity.
Nothing was born;
Nothing will die;
All things will change.

"Juba"

"Juba" was a patting song sung by slaves. There are many theories about its name and origin. One source says that the Juba dance takes its name from a West African dance called "djouba," brought here by slaves. Another claims that "Juba" is short for the word "jubilee."

Patting means clapping, or slapping one's thighs, chest, or knees. Slaves often didn't have instruments, and according to some sources, they were forbidden from having drums, lest those drums be used to communicate in secret code over distances and incite local rebellions. So instead, slaves often "patted" their own rhythms, and Juba became very popular.

Juba, Juba,
Juba up 'n' Juba down,
Juba all over the town.
Juba, Juba,
Juba this 'n' Juba that,
Juba killed the yaller cat.
Juba, Juba,
Juba left 'n' Juba right,
Juba, Juba, gettin' night.

"Motherless Children Sees a Hard Time"

This was a religious song sung by slaves in the South. The lyrics as sung
by Zipporah Tweed were changed and softened from the original lyrics
written below.

Motherless children sees a hard time when mother is dead.

Motherless children sees a hard time when mother is dead.

Here they go run from door to door,

Yes, they have nowhere to go.

Motherless children sees a hard time when mother is dead.

Some people say your father will do when mother is dead.

Some people say father will do when mother is dead.

Some people say father will do.

Soon as he get married turn his back on you.

Nobody treat you like mother will when mother is dead.

Some people say your older sister will do when your
      mother is dead.

Some people say older sister will do when mother is dead.

Some people say your sister will do.

Soon as she get married, she turn her back on you.

Nobody treat you like mother will when mother is dead.

I said, motherless children sees a hard time when mother is
      dead. *(Lord, Lord.)*

Motherless children sees a hard time when mother is dead.

Father will do the best he can,

But, you know, father can't understand.

Nobody treat you like your mother will when mother
    is dead.

"Brother, Can You Spare a Dime"

This is the song that the taxi driver at the New Orleans train station was listening to on his car radio. During the Depression, millions of Americans lost their jobs and homes. This song, which was recorded in 1931, reflected the hopelessness and anger many of them felt.

They used to tell me I was building a dream, and so I
    followed the mob,
When there was earth to plow, or guns to bear, I was always
    there right on the job.
They used to tell me I was building a dream, with peace
    and glory ahead,
Why should I be standing in line, just waiting for bread?

Once I built a railroad, I made it run, made it race against
    time.
Once I built a railroad; now it's done. Brother, can you
    spare a dime?
Once I built a tower, up to the sun, brick, and rivet, and
    lime;
Once I built a tower, now it's done. Brother, can you spare
    a dime?

Once in khaki suits, gee we looked swell,
Full of that Yankee Doodly Dum,

Half a million boots went slogging through Hell,
And I was the kid with the drum!

Say, don't you remember, they called me Al; it was Al all
    the time.
Why don't you remember, I'm your pal? Buddy, can you
    spare a dime?

Once in khaki suits, gee we looked swell,
Full of that Yankee Doodly Dum,
Half a million boots went slogging through Hell,
And I was the kid with the drum!

Say, don't you remember, they called me Al; it was Al all
    the time.
Say, don't you remember, I'm your pal? Buddy, can you
    spare a dime?

"Aunt Maria"

This folk song, also sung by Zipporah Tweed to Tennyson, was another
"patting song."

Old Aunt Maria, jump in the fire.

Fire too hot, jump in the pot.

Pot too black, jump in the crack.

Crack too high, jump in the sky.

Sky too blue, jump in canoe.

Canoe too shallow, jump in the tallow.

Tallow too soft, jump in the loft.

Loft too rotten, jump in the cotton.

Cotton so white, she stay there all night.

ACKNOWLEDGMENTS

Without Caitlin Baldwin Crounse, this book would not exist, and that is why it is dedicated to her. There is barely a paragraph that does not bear her imprint in one way or another. Without her, I never would have known about Sally Mann or Southern rivers or night fishing—all of the things that really matter.

The loss of her family's house in Pass Christian, Mississippi, during Hurricane Katrina felt like a death in my own family and reminded me that in the South, all things will change, usually brutally. My love and gratitude toward her and her family run deeper than I can express.

***

I am also extremely thankful to my editor at Knopf, Erin Clarke, whose emotional involvement in this project was on a par with my own. The same goes for my agent, Christine Earle, whose support has been tireless.

Thank you also to Gregory Macek, who will be my husband by the time this book goes to print. He was wonderfully tolerant of my extended emotional stay at Aigredoux, which makes for an interesting home life, I can assure you.

As usual, my mother commands much gratitude for her involvement. We drove all over southern Louisiana and Mississippi together as I researched this project. I'm sure that neither of us will ever forget the night we stayed alone in a haunted plantation house overlooking the Mississippi River, with only a peacock named Napoleon to keep us company.

And on that note, I would also like to thank the staffs at the following plantations for their tours and help with my research: Dunleith, the Myrtles, Oak Alley, Monmouth, Houmas, Destrehan, Ormond, the Briars Inn, Nottoway, and Longwood. I am particularly indebted to Jay at the Laura plantation and Catherine at the San Francisco plantation. Their knowledge of and passion for local history gave me endless inspiration as I wrote this book.